LOVE AND GIRAFFES

JAIME W. POWELL

www.cleanreads.com

Love and Giraffes
by Jaime Powell
Published by Clean Reads
www.cleanreads.com

LOVE AND GIRAFFES
Copyright © 2018 JAIME POWELL
ISBN 978-1-62135-790-2
Cover Art Designed by AM DESIGNS STUDIO

For J.J.
Ours is my favorite love story.

1

BRETT

ARRIVING HERE IS like admitting defeat. All other options have been exhausted. This place is for the most broken of the broken, the most desperate of the desperate. But I'm not entirely convinced I'm desperate or broken enough to be here. I glance through the window and see myself in the people mingling around the dimly lit tables for two. A part of me wants to think I'm better than this, above it even—above the humiliation, the nervousness, and the desperation. Here I am, though, thanks to my supposed best friend, Phil.

"This isn't necessary," I say, pushing my hand against the door as Phil tries to open it.

"Look, man. This is what single people do. I know you've been out of the loop for a few years, but if you want to meet women, this is the quickest way to do it. You've been divorced for two years. Time to get back in the game." I stare at him, not entirely sold on the idea. "Brett, let go of the door, straighten your jacket, and man up."

"Speed dating, though? This is the most ridiculous thing I've ever done. Can't people meet organically anymore?" I drop my hand from the door and adjust my jacket.

"Nowadays this *is* organic, and you forget — we went to college together. This is nowhere near the most ridiculous thing you've ever done. I'm pretty sure the porn star wax one of your old flames talked you into trumps this," he laughs.

I smirk and shake my head as we enter. "I was drunk."

"You were whipped."

"I'm not having this conversation with you right now. Or ever, for that matter. Besides, I didn't do everything she asked me to," I remind him.

"Yeah, you certainly put your foot down, and I thought we weren't having this discussion."

"I did, and we're not."

"Fine," he says as we take a seat at the bar. I order my usual whisky and cola and Phil settles for a White Russian.

"So, how does this work?" I ask.

"I don't know. I've never been."

"Then how do you even know about this place?"

"How do you *not*? You own a bar. Half the people who leave here together wind up at your bar, and I end up serving them," he says, taking a swig of his drink as he peers around the candlelit room. There are several small, round tables in the crowded room of relationship hopefuls. Each one is lit with a small candle set inside a red holder, giving the room a romantic glow.

As I observe the room, I can't help but notice that most are here with a friend. Apparently, Phil and I aren't the only ones who didn't want to come alone.

"Hello everyone, and welcome to speed dating!" a middle-aged woman announces over a microphone. As she spits out the rules to the dating game, I see Phil is already winking at a slender woman in a blue, silk top, and she is flirtatiously smiling back. This guy has never met a stranger. I scan the room but notice no one I want to start winking at. "After four minutes, the

2

buzzer will go off, and gentleman, we ask that you move on to the next table."

As I table jump through the night, I let the women do most of the talking. I occasionally glance over at Phil and see him caressing a woman's hand or duck in close to whisper something to them. This seems to be much more his scene than mine. I listen to twenty-year-olds talk about how their exes burned them and forty-year-olds talk about their kids and ex-husbands, and by the time the buzzer buzzes for the last table, I am all too ready to leave.

I sit at the last table, and the woman staring back at me is stone-faced. Her hands cradle her drink on the table, and she's chewing the inside of her cheek.

"Hi. I'm Brett," I say for the hundredth time tonight.

"Quinn."

"Quinn. Beautiful name. So, what do you do for a living, Quinn?"

She glares up from her glass, narrowing her eyes at me. "Do you care?"

I wonder for a moment if her job is a sore subject for her, but there's something about her demeanor that tells me she's in the same boat I'm in. Though, where I can hide my annoyance, she cannot.

"No. No, I don't care." We share a moment, staring at one another. "You don't want to be here."

She smirks with raised brows. "No, I don't."

I sigh in relief. "Yeah, me neither. So, do you just want to sit in silence for the next three minutes or would you rather tell me why you're here then?"

"Well, why are *you* here?" she asks.

"I was dragged here kicking and screaming by my friend, Phil, over there," I say nodding my head in his direction.

"Oh, him," she says knowingly. "Yeah, he's a real charmer.

Or at least he thinks he is."

I chuckle. "He likes to flirt."

"Yeah, with anything that has breasts it seems."

"So, I take it you were dragged here as well."

"Yeah. My friend, Fran," she says motioning to a blonde in a purple strapless shirt who is currently chatting it up with a salt-and-pepper-haired man.

"Yeah, I spoke with her earlier. Nice girl." I stare at Quinn's long brown hair and her emerald-green eyes and wonder how I missed her when I was scanning the crowd. She's quite lovely. I'm also a little relieved to see she's a wee bit ticked off and not buying into this speed dating trap like the other women seem to be doing. "This is the most honest conversation I've had tonight, and the most relaxed."

Her eyes narrow again for a second. "What did you expect to get out of this tonight?"

I purse my lips together and slowly shake my head. "Nothing. I'm not looking for a relationship."

She smirks. "I'm not either. What do you say after that buzzer goes off, the four of us go get a bite to eat."

I tilt my head and grin. "Why?"

"My treat," she says.

I can't help but be intrigued. Why does she want to have dinner with me if she's not looking to date? Why is she dodging the question for that matter? Now the buzzer sounds.

She scribbles something on the back of a card from her purse and hands it to me. "That's my number. There's an Italian place just three blocks from here. Fran and I will be there if you decide to come."

"Okay." I watch her friend meet her at the door, not staying for a second longer. I suppose her friend didn't meet the man of her dreams either then. Speed daters. I shake my head.

"Oh! You got a number!" Phil exclaims, joining me at

my side.

"Actually, I got a date. I think."

"Seriously? When?"

"Now."

He laughs. "Well, don't let me stop you."

"I'm not. You're going with me," I say.

"Wait. Huh? Why am I going on your date?"

"I'm guessing because it's a double date. She came here with a friend. She wants the four of us to eat at some Italian place three blocks from here."

"I'm down," he says with a clap of his hands.

I'm completely intrigued by my exchange with Quinn. I decide to go, as if I'm being led by some cosmic force beyond my understanding.

————

AS WE TURN the corner of West 14th Street the restaurant comes into view. Green plants outline a white brick half wall around the quaint, cottage restaurant. A wooden door with an archway leads us into the poorly lit eatery where I see Quinn and her friend, Fran, looking over their menus.

"Ah, man. *That's* her friend?" he asks.

"Yeah, why? She's gorgeous. What do you have to complain about?"

"Yeah, she's gorgeous all right, and completely stuck-up."

"Why's that?" I ask.

He smooths his hair and fiddles nervously with his collar. "Let's just say I won't be asking for her number again."

I laugh as the hostess leads us to the table. "You mean she wasn't buying into your game."

"Hey. You have your charm, she has her beauty, and I have my game. We all use what God gives us."

"So, you made it," Quinn says.

"Yeah. Quinn this is Phil. Phil, Quinn."

"Pleasure to meet you," he says to Quinn as he kisses her hand. I roll my eyes.

"Nice. Okay," Quinn says, pulling her hand back. "You guys remember Fran, I'm sure."

"I do. Nice to see you again," I say, sliding into the booth seat.

"Fran," says Phil.

"Hello again," she says.

As the waiter takes our drink orders, I see Quinn looking me up and down as if I'm a calculus problem that she's deciphering. We all sit for a short time glancing through the menu. The silence is deafening at first. But soon we begin to make small talk about the lovely Manhattan weather, and Phil compliments the ladies on their choice of restaurant. The whole time we're talking, I get the distinct impression that Fran doesn't know why we are there any more than we do.

"Did you guys enjoy speed dating?" Fran asks.

"It was... different," I admit.

"A room full of single ladies? I loved it," Phil says.

I smile apologetically. "Obviously, it was his idea." I nod toward him. Quinn has barely said a word. She doesn't strike me as the shy type. Reserved maybe, but not shy.

The waiter brings over four glasses of wine the ladies must have ordered before we arrived. Great. More cheap liquor. Just what Phil needs.

"So, Quinn," I say, "you asked us here."

She nods. "Yes, I did."

I glance around. "You don't want a relationship. Are you just looking for friendship?"

She shakes her head. "No, I'm looking for sex."

"Wow," says Phil.

"Check!" hollers Fran.

"Sex," I say. She nods. "Well, you picked a nice place for it."

She laughs through her nose.

"Quinn has had one too many glasses of wine tonight," Fran says. "She doesn't know what she's saying."

"I know what I'm saying," she says. "Look, I see myself in you. You've been burned. You don't buy into the dating game any more than I do. I've dated. I've walked down the aisle. I've played the game. Now I just want sex.

"I want a guy I can call up at three in the morning for it. I want a guy I can meet in random places for it. I want to have fun."

I glance to Phil and his mouth hangs open. Reaching over, I push it closed. Fran has her face hidden behind her hand as she takes a large drink from her wine.

"Is that supposed to be where I come in?" I ask.

"If you want," she says.

I see Phil peek at Fran and wiggle his eyebrows. "No," she says.

I laugh. Quinn can't be serious. She just met me. She doesn't even know my last name. Is she crazy?

"Why would I agree to something like that? I just met you," I remind her.

"Why wouldn't you?" she asks. "A no-strings attached sex partner that you can call up any time, day or night, and have sex with."

The waiter brings the check, and as Fran signs the receipt, Quinn and I stare at one another. I can't decide which would be crazier: agreeing or turning her down. She's a beautiful woman, and for a moment, I wonder what has happened in her life to make her pull such a stunt.

As Fran scoots Quinn from the booth, Quinn glances at me one last time. "You have my number."

―――――

"YOU LUCKY DOG!" Phil says, throwing his arm around my shoulder as we walk home together.

"Am I? You don't think that was a little crazy?"

"Yeah. Crazy lucky. She's hot."

"Yeah, hot," I mumble. I put my hands in my pants pockets and feel the card she gave me there. I take it out. It's an appointment card of some sort with an expired date on one side, and on the other is simply her first name and her number. No last name, so no way of looking her up online or even in a phone book.

I arrive at my apartment building and wave goodbye to Phil, telling him I'll see him in the morning at work. I own a bar, Brett's Bar, and he's been one of my bartenders for three years now. He met me right after I married my wife, while attending college, and he saw me through my divorce and all the ugliness in-between. In his eyes, I hit pay dirt tonight—a lovely woman willing to fulfill my every sexual desire. To me, there must be something more to a relationship than just sex.

Can I do that? Can I take advantage of a woman in this way? Can I use a woman strictly for sex and walk away an hour later? Is that what she truly wants?

She said she's walked down the aisle, so she's been married. I'm guessing that the marriage wasn't the best if it left her only wanting to use men and not love them, but has my marriage left me wanting the same of women?

Maybe. Maybe this is just what I need right now, too. A playmate. Someone to have fun with. A pal that I get to have sex with.

She is beautiful though. She has a soccer mom look to her. Underneath everything, she seems like the kind of woman I'd bring home to my mom. Wait—maybe I can.

2

QUINN

"YOU KNOW you're out of your mind, right?" Fran says as we watch the girls practice their fielding. "You're a member of the community. You're a high school softball coach. If your actions from last night got around to the parents of these girls, what do you think they would do?"

I laugh. "The married ones or the divorced ones?"

"Not funny. You don't know this guy, Quinn. He could be a crazy person, for all you know."

"For all he knows, I could be a crazy person."

"Well after last night, that's a distinct possibility."

I take a break from Fran's lecturing to assist one of the girls on her batting stance while Fran makes her way to the pitcher to work on her release. She's probably right about me. I probably have gone crazy, but my personal life is no one's business but my own.

What's wrong with a thirty-year-old looking for a little fun after her divorce? What's the difference between what I put on the table for Brett and going out to the bars on the weekends and having one-night stands after a night of loose drinking? The difference is I make the rules, and I don't get hurt.

I don't walk away from a one-night stand with some romantic notion that it will turn out to be more. At least my way no one gets hurt, and everyone is happy. I make no promises, and I expect no promises. That's the way life has to be now.

"Remember, for all you know, this guy could be a serial killer, right?" Fran says as we meet back on the third base line.

"If that's true, it would be your fault."

"Oh, I can't wait to hear this."

"Well, speed dating was your idea, right? So even if he and I just agreed to date and he eventually killed me, it would be no different."

She stares at the field with her arms crossed. "It's sickening the way your mind works. You know that, right?"

I chuckle. "I think his friend Phil has a thing for you."

"His friend Phil has a thing for himself. Not interested." She yells out to one of the girls to pay attention before refocusing on me. "Have you even given any thought to Evie? Or have you forgotten that you have an eight-year-old at home?"

"This conversation is getting old."

"I'm serious. Think about the example you're setting."

"I'm not exactly going to be inviting Evie to come along, Fran. She won't even know he exists, and he won't know she exists."

"Oh, that's starting a relationship on the right foot."

"You don't get it! It's not going to be a relationship. It's sex. You can have one without the other, you know?"

"Well, that remains to be seen. Have you told Thomas about this yet?

"When would I have told him? The only person I've been with in the past twelve hours is you."

———

TONIGHT, I invited Fran and Thomas, my best friend, over for a painting party with wine and pizza. I promised Evie we would paint ladybugs on her bedroom walls while she's away at her dad's. Ladybugs are by far her favorite, and I've been looking for ways to make this new condo feel more like home to her ever since my divorce. It doesn't take long for Fran to delve into my "free sex campaign" as she calls it.

"We've seriously been in the restaurant for five minutes, and she's offering some strange man sex!"

"Honestly, I'm not sure whose side to be on here." Thomas laughs. "Fran, I hear what you're saying, and I don't necessarily agree with Quinn's choices, but Quinn," he says, glancing back at me, "I commend you on your ability to know what you want. Too many women are searching for love in all the wrong places —speed dating being one of them." He gives Fran a raised eyebrow. "She's not acting like a crazy person — she's just acting like a man," he chuckles.

"See," I say to Fran, "all I'm doing is what every man has done to a woman at some point—had sex with her just for the fun of it. The only difference is I'm being upfront about it and not asking for a call the next day. Easy-peasy."

"So, did he agree to it?" he asks.

"I don't know. I haven't heard from him yet."

"Yeah, probably because you scared him," Fran mutters.

"I doubt that," Thomas says. "He's probably just not sure how to go about accepting the proposal. I know I'd be stumped."

"Well, I'm not worried about it. He'll come around or he won't. There's plenty of men out there who would jump at the offer," I say as I finish a big, black dot on one of the ladybug's backs. I leave the room to rinse out my brush, and as I watch the water run through the black paint, I begin to question myself.

Is what I offered so wrong? Was I being as ridiculous as Fran thinks? I squeeze the bristles in my hand and watch the gray liquid squish through my fingers. I turn the water off and stare out the kitchen window above the sink.

Maybe she was right. I do have an eight-year-old I need to think about. No, no. I'm a grown woman, and I'm not doing anything wrong. Many women with children date numerous men or sleep around. I'm not doing either.

I'm choosing one man that can see me through a tough day without either of us feeling pressured to make a commitment of some sort. I'm not ready to date, but I am a red-blooded woman who has needs, and sometimes a woman needs a man to make love to her. There's nothing wrong with that. It's human nature.

I could have made the offer to Thomas. Thomas is a handsome man, tall with dark hair and eyes. I can see why women are attracted to him, and it seems he always has a new lady on his arm.

But I just can't think of him that way. I've known him too long. He's the guy I call to go shopping with me or have over for pizza and painting, like tonight. Not the sort of man I call randomly for sex, and I doubt he's the kind of guy that would agree to such anyways.

Whether he would admit to it or not, he's the sort that wants to settle down with a family. It just always seems like he sabotages his relationships in one way or another. It also doesn't help that Fran and I are his best friends. Apparently, most girls are threatened by a man with girls as friends. I suppose since my divorce, I can see why.

As I walk back to the bedroom, I hear whispering, but I can't make out what's being said. I have a feeling, though, that it's Fran trying to convince Thomas to talk me out of all of this. I can't say that I blame her. I might be doing the same thing if the roles were reversed.

"You can stop talking about me now," I say, entering the room.

"My turn," Fran says, picking up her paintbrush and heading for the kitchen. I'm sure she's taking this time to let Thomas talk to me. I don't mind. I value his input, especially his male point of view.

"So, lecture me, Thomas. I know it's coming." I dip my brush in white paint to begin a large cloud on the pale blue wall of the room.

"No, I'm not going to lecture you."

"It's fine. I'd like to know what you think."

"What I think? I think you're lonely and afraid of getting hurt."

I continue to swipe the paint onto the wall without making eye contact.

"But, don't you think Fran might have a little bit of a point? Not so much about you randomly asking a guy for sex, but maybe you just need to date. There are good guys out there."

"I know there are," I say. "So, maybe I am afraid of getting hurt, but maybe loosening up is just what I need. I wasn't alluring enough for Spencer, apparently."

"That's what this is about, isn't it? Your loser husband cheats on you, and suddenly you think you are undesirable. So, instead of putting your heart out there, you just decide to put your body out there?"

Is that why I'm doing this? Yes, I'm afraid of getting hurt, but am I only doing this because my ex-husband cheated on me? I drop my hand from the wall and sit on the floor, plopping my brush down and grabbing my glass of wine and taking a large gulp. "So, what if it is? Is that so wrong? I loved that man since I met him at seventeen, and then one day he just decided I wasn't good enough for him anymore and began seeing a stripper. I'm entitled to a little fun now that it's all over."

"Quinn, don't sell yourself short."

"I'm not. I just... I need a male presence in my life without the drama. Spencer and I had been together for so long that I don't know anything else. I've cooked and cleaned and been a mother my whole adult life. So, now I just need a man I can call when I *need* a man, but I'm not ready for another relationship, and I'm not ready to bring some new guy into Evie's life."

"I understand that. I just don't want to see you get hurt. Believe it or not, you can still get hurt in a no-strings attached situation."

"I don't see how. No promises mean no let downs."

"Oh, sweetie, you can always get hurt. Men will always find a way to hurt women without even meaning to, and women will always do the same to men. Especially with you." He mutters the last under his breath.

"And what is that supposed to mean?"

"Honey, some people can do the no-strings attached game and some can't. I know you. If you start spending any kind of time alone with this man and he ends up being a good guy, you'll fall for him. And who could blame you after being with Spencer all those years? First time I saw you two together, I knew it wasn't going to end pretty."

"Oh, you knew? Please explain."

"He didn't treat you like an equal. Everyone could see that. He saw himself above you and obviously still does."

I pick the pepperoni off a piece of pizza. Not because I don't like pepperoni, but because I refuse to make eye contact now. Mostly because I know he's right.

"Do you truly think you can have sex with a man regularly without becoming attached?" Fran asks from the doorway, having apparently heard the majority of our conversation.

I gaze up at her. "Yeah, I think I can. Too many people confuse sex with love. I'm not one of them, though." I watch Fran and Thomas exchange a glance before there's a knock at the door.

I take my time walking to answer the door as a sad attempt at trying to abstain from the conversation. Unfortunately, I know my ex-husband is on the other side.

"Hey, baby!" I say, grabbing Evie up into a bear hug. "Thank you for being on time," I tell Spencer.

"Of course. Um, Melissa wanted to ask if she could take Evie out for a movie one night this week. Just to get to know her a little better," he says. My heart sinks. The woman who stole my husband wants to be alone with my child.

I knew this day would come, and I knew it would be soon, but there's a break in my heart that is indescribable. I can see from the expression on Spencer's face just how hard it was to ask me this. Despite his past actions, he is a good father and a good person. I know this.

"We'll see," is all I can manage to choke out.

"Thanks, Quinn." He peeks down at Evie. "Daddy will see you later, baby girl."

"Bye, Daddy!" she says.

I force a smile and close the door, putting my back to it and wanting to sink into the ground.

I didn't realize how much I missed Spencer's face until now. I miss his thick brown hair and dark blue eyes. I miss his trimmed beard and the smell of his cologne, and now some other woman is sleeping next to him every night. How did my life manage to do such a one-eighty?

"Uncle Thomas! Aunt Fran!" Evie calls out.

"Hey, Bug!" Thomas calls out. Thomas has called her "Bug" ever since she was born. Perhaps that's why she took a liking to ladybugs early on. Fran has since joined in on the nickname fun. "Come see your room. It's not finished yet, but it's getting there," he says, recognizing I need a minute to myself.

I go to the bathroom, tie my hair back, splash water on my face, and stare at my own reflection. My green eyes seem more piercing than usual, and I remember Fran telling me once that when I'm upset, it seems my eyes change colors, although I don't believe that.

I remember our wedding video and how young I looked at the tender age of twenty. My hair was shiny, there were no lines on my face, and I had my whole life in front of me with the man I thought I would spend it with. Now I gaze in the mirror, and though I'm still young, I see the ten years of marriage in the dark circles around my eyes and the frown lines around my mouth. Still an attractive woman, but aged nonetheless. I am now broken.

I can't start a new relationship. I can't even date. I need to find myself again. I need to figure out what I want and who I am, and I think good friends, wine, pizza, painting, and a healthy sex life is a good place to start.

3

BRETT

GLANCING down at Quinn's card on my dresser, I button my shirt and get ready to head to the bar. It's been two days since our little encounter, and I suppose I can see why Quinn chose me from the crowd. I'm always well-dressed and well-groomed. Many people don't take pride in the way they look anymore, as I do.

I have dark skin from working in the sun as a young man for years and have dark eyes and hair to match. Some days I've been described as a preppy guy, and on days when I have chosen not to shave, a few have called me rugged. I suppose I'm an equal mix.

I'm sure by now Phil has filled in the whole group on the goings on. To him, I've struck gold. Maybe I have. I think, despite the craziness of this whole ordeal, Quinn has something I need, just as I have something she needs. What are relationships other than filling gaps for another person, be it friendship, marriage, or in this case a sex partner, anyway? I hastily shove the card in my wallet.

"THERE HE IS!" Phil calls out as I enter the front door of Brett's Bar, my high-end bar on the upper east side of Manhattan. High-end maybe, but most of my clientele are regular customers who frequent the bar after work each day or on dates. Apparently, some are even speed daters, from what Phil says.

The place is well-lit with the neon beer signs and the neon blue light under the bar top. Even our serving trays are outlined in neon lights. Small, round tables for two take up the center of the room with booths outlining the perimeter. Phil and Kara are behind the bar tonight, and Janine is serving drinks in the next room to those who are entertaining themselves with friendly games of pool.

Janine and Kara have been here since the bar opened. They are each gorgeous in their own way, each with flowing golden hair, though Kara has long legs while Janine is quite petite. They keep the male customers in their seats. Phil, on the other hand, has his own fan base. The ladies swoon over him. They all love his charming personality, and he loves the ladies. *Any* ladies. They can be tall, short, thin, thick, old, or young. He loves them all.

Janine tends to flirt with the customers, whereas Kara is usually strictly business. Mostly, though, Janine flirts with me. I'm not interested. I'm thirty-five years old and she's barely twenty-two.

Not that age is a huge factor for me. It's not. I consider myself a young guy, but I tend to understand how much older I am when I'm around her and her friends.

I sometimes feel like I'm still in my twenties, to be honest, until I hang around people in their twenties. Then I'm reminded.

"Kara, can you hold down the fort? I need Phil's help outside," I say.

"Yup," she answers.

We walk outside where white lights hang from a canopied awning. White lights also adorn the trunks of the surrounding trees, and the customers seem to love all the little extras. It makes the bar feel classy.

I've always had a nose for business and can tell what the public enjoys. I'm constantly doing little upgrades to make sure we stay ahead of our competitors. I lead Phil to the tables in the back of the patio that still need to be set for the band due to play tonight.

"What band is playing tonight?" Phil asks as we throw decorative cloths over the small, black metal tables.

I point to a dry erase board that rests on an easel beside the makeshift stage. "The Blue Man Blues."

"Never heard of 'em."

"Just a local band looking for a place to play regularly. I told the guys I'd give them a shot tonight. So, I take it Kara and Janine already know about everything?"

"Why do you say that?"

"Well, because Janine isn't up my butt right now."

He laughs. "Well, maybe she's just busy."

"Or maybe you're horrible about gossiping."

"Well, that could be it, too." He chuckles. "Why have you never given her a chance anyways? So, she's a little younger than you. So, what? She worships you."

"Because she reminds me of a younger version of my ex-wife."

"Your ex-wife was a gold digging nightmare."

"Exactly, and I'm not in the market for another one."

Janine only 'worships' me because she is infatuated with me. She sees a young guy with his own successful business. She doesn't see *me*. It was the same with my ex-wife. She only saw beach getaways, the Hope Diamond of an engagement ring I presented her with, and extra zeroes in her checking account.

le myself on being a smart guy, but I never even saw
et coming. Maybe it was because I was infatuated with
her, too. She was gorgeous, a tiger in the bedroom, and a lady in
public. Sounds like a dream, but it wasn't. Like Phil said, she
was a nightmare.

———

"SO, WHAT'S SHE LIKE?" Kara says, slapping a coaster and
beer in front of me as I sit at the bar, having finished outside.

I grimace. "Is nothing sacred with you people?"

"C'mon, c'mon. It's not every day a woman just picks you
out of a crowd and offers you unlimited sex. Did you expect
word not to travel around here? You know this bar is worse than
a small town." I watch Janine swipe a rag from behind the bar
and storm off. "She'll get over it," Kara says. "So, tell me what
she's like."

"What can I tell you that Phil hasn't already told you?"
I laugh.

"What do you think of her?"

"Well..."

"I can tell you something," Janine chimes in as she shuffles
back into the room, as though she had never left. "She's
damaged goods. Any woman who offers herself like that is either
damaged or has ulterior motives." She quickly walks away.

"Brett, it's not often that Janine and I are in agreement, but
something's wrong with this woman."

"If a guy made the same offer to a woman, you'd just say he
was a douche bag. That being said, I think she's been hurt in the
past. She mentioned a marriage before."

"Well yeah, you've been married, too, but I don't see you
pimping yourself out on Main Street."

"True, but what ulterior motive could she have? She doesn't know me."

"I don't know, but I'd be careful to find out if I were you."

———

AS THE BAND PLAYS TONIGHT, I stand in the back, watching Janine flirt with the customers and Kara wipe down the bar inside. Phil, on the other hand, I see stuff a tip in his pants pocket and head toward me with a goofy smile on his face.

"If you bring up Quinn right now, I'll kill you. I've heard enough about her tonight."

"Yeah," he laughs. "That's not going to be easy." He nods toward the patio door as Quinn makes her way outside and sits at a table to watch the band with her friend, Fran. She doesn't seem to have noticed me.

"What?" I ask.

"I don't know, dude. Maybe the girls were right. If she knows this is your bar, she might be a stalker or just think you're rich."

"Phil, I *am* rich."

"My point exactly."

"How would she know this is my bar?"

"Maybe because your name is in the title," he laughs.

"Right, because obviously, I'm the only Brett in Manhattan?"

"So, you think this is all coincidence?"

I stare at Quinn and notice her wave to the drummer and he returns a nod. I smirk. "Yeah, I think it is," I say pointing to their exchange.

He laughs. "Maybe that's another fish she has on the hook."

I shake my head, wondering the same thing, but something

about their acknowledgment of each other makes me think they aren't in that kind of relationship.

"I'm going to go talk to them," Phil says.

"No," I say, catching his arm, "wait."

He peeks around. "What are we waiting for?"

"Just wait until the band goes on break. I want to see them together."

Half an hour has passed, and I now see Phil pointing out Quinn to Kara. I roll my eyes as I hear the band announce a fifteen-minute break. The drummer stands up and stretches before making his way to Quinn's table. They hug and he sits down with her and Fran.

"What are you going to do?" Kara asks, suddenly at my side.

"What's she drinking?" I ask.

"Long Island."

"Send her one on me. Courtesy of the handsome man at the bar."

Kara grins. "Yes, sir."

"What are you up to?" Phil asks.

I grin. "I want to see her reaction when she sees me. If she already knew it was my bar, I'll be able to tell."

Kara takes her tray with a single drink on it, and I see her place the drink on the table and point in my direction. Quinn turns, and her eyes dart around until they find me. Her face drops, and I see the drummer ask her a question. She shakes her head and refocuses on her friends. Not the reaction I was expecting. It's obvious she didn't know it was my bar when she got here, but I bet she's putting two and two together right now.

She stands with her purse and heads inside the bar as she eyes me, beckoning me to follow. I set my beer on the table nearest me and walk quickly to meet up with her. She stops near the restroom openings and rushes me with a hasty wave of her hand.

"What are you doing here?" she asks.

"You're kidding, right?" Her eyes are wide. She seriously has no idea. "Brett's Bar. In case you didn't hear me in the midst of throwing yourself at me, I'm Brett."

"Oh, no." She ducks her head. "I feel so stupid."

"Yeah, well..."

"Well, you can't be the man I threw myself at tonight, okay? You're just some guy who bought me a drink."

"What are you talking about? What? Is the drummer another one of your lovers?"

Her eyes roll. "I'm not a whore."

"Never said you were. Just wondering why I'm a secret tonight when you were so forthcoming two nights ago."

"Because my brother is here!"

"What? What do you mean? The drummer?"

"Yes. The drummer. Oh, no. Here he comes. Randy!" she says.

"Hey, I didn't know you knew the owner," he says.

"Oh, well she didn't until now. I saw her across the crowd and had to introduce myself. She tells me you're her brother."

"Yeah, last time I checked," he jokes.

Quinn laughs nervously, followed by awkward silence.

"Well, I got to get back to overseeing things. It was nice to meet you, Quinn. And Randy, you guys sound great. Keep it up and I'll have to have you out again soon."

"Sounds great, man," he says, shaking my hand once more. I walk off as Quinn enters the bathroom, and Randy waits his turn. What a small world. I hired her brother, and she obviously had no idea this was my bar.

I can say one thing for her, she doesn't seem like a gold digger. That conversation could have easily gone a different way. She could have acted like she and I were best buds or even dating, but she didn't. She didn't even want her brother to know that we knew one another.

Maybe she truly was only wanting a sex life. I'm way more intrigued now than I was an hour ago. Honestly, I want to use this card in my pocket now. I want to call her and talk to her. Janine was worried that she had an ulterior motive, but if I'm being honest, I have one now.

"What was that all about?" Phil asks as Kara rushes over to hear.

"She didn't know it was my place, and the drummer? It's her *brother*." They both gasp with laughter.

"You're kidding me," he says.

"I kid you not."

"Small world," Kara chimes in.

"Yeah. I think I'm going to do it."

"What do you mean? Nail her?" he asks.

My shoulders slump, and my eyes find the floor. "Phil, you have zero class."

"Okay. Okay. I mean *make love* to her?" he says sarcastically.

"Phil, you're such a jerk," says Kara.

"Don't you people have jobs to do or something? Serve a drink. Wipe down a table. Do something, for goodness sake," I order as I walk off.

———

THE NIGHT CLOSES with the band loading up their equipment, the customers paying their tabs, and Quinn and Fran slipping out the door without so much as a goodbye. Janine hasn't said anything to me tonight, but anytime my eyes cross her path, she quickly looks away from me. I would feel bad if I had given her false hope, but I never have.

"You should talk to her," Kara says from behind me, as I chunk empty bottles in the garbage.

I shake my head. "What would I even say? 'I'm sorry you're in love me, and I might sleep with someone else'?"

"Take it from a woman, Brett. It's not easy seeing a guy you're into date someone else. You know how she feels."

"Then maybe you guys shouldn't have told her what was going on."

"Hey, talk to Phil about that. You shouldn't have to hide your relationships anyway. No matter what kind of relationship it is."

I raise my head to the sky and close my eyes in frustration, but she's right. The girl is hurt. I *should* talk to her. She's cleaning on the opposite side of the bar, on purpose I'm sure, as I walk over to her. I start helping her bus a table, but she never looks up.

"Tell me what's on your mind. You can't keep avoiding eye contact with me."

She shakes her head and never looks up. "I haven't been avoiding anything."

I lean my head down to peek at her. "You're still doing it."

She drops a wet rag on the table and places a hand on her hip. "Is that all you want? Someone to have sex with?"

I tilt my head. "Kind of a personal question, Janine."

She shakes her head with a sarcastic chuckle. "Come on, Brett. You've discussed this with Phil and Kara all night, but when I ask, it's too personal? Don't treat me like a child."

"You're right," I say. "I shouldn't treat you like a child, but trust me when I say I haven't wanted it discussed at all, even with them. They just happen to be pushier than you, and nosier, actually."

"Does this mean you're not going to answer the question?"

I lick my lips. "Look, I know... I know how you feel about

25

me, but you're young. You're going to feel this way about a lot of guys before you find the right one."

She snickers. "So, that's that then, right?"

"Janine, I care about you, but..."

"But it was never going to happen. I know. I know you all think I'm young, and yeah, I am. That doesn't make any of you smarter than me. Mark my words, if you call her, it won't stop with sex. You're too good of a guy to use a woman that way. It may start with it, but it won't end with it. Someone will fall in love, or someone will get hurt, or both."

I swallow hard at her words.

4

QUINN

SEEING Brett at the bar would have been a welcome experience if my family hadn't been the source of entertainment for the night. Only *I* could have created such a mess for myself. But I suppose something good came from it. He called me this morning, and now I'm about to meet him at the coffee shop around the corner.

As I arrive, I see he has saved us a table by the window. Good. Having a window to gaze out of gives me a strange sort of comfort.

"Quinn," he says, standing as I arrive at the table.

"Hey." It's all I manage to choke out. I'm nervous. When did that happen? I was so brazen the night we met. Of course, I was full of cheap alcohol and had Fran as an ally.

"I didn't know what kind of coffee you like, so I just ordered you what I like. I hope it's okay."

"It's fine. Sorry about all the secrecy last night, but I appreciate you being discrete."

"It wasn't a problem. Of course, had I known it was your brother at the table, I wouldn't have sent a drink over to you," he says.

I laugh. "It's okay. He never even mentioned it."

"Good."

"So, I'm guessing since you asked me here, you've considered my offer," I say with a slight wince, though he doesn't seem to notice. I hate to make it sound like a business proposition, but what else is it?

"Uh, yeah, I have."

"And?" I take a swig of coffee, afraid of the answer for the first time. Three days ago, I was sure what I wanted.

"And I have a condition."

I swallow. "A condition? Are you under the impression you're my only choice?" With his remark, I suddenly have my confidence back.

He laughs. "You asked me for a reason. I don't know what your reason was, but there were plenty of other guys you could have chosen. Now, if you want to go speed dating again to find yourself another lover, you can go right ahead, or you can listen to what I have to say. You might like what you hear."

My brows push together. "Fine. What is it?"

"My parents arrange a week-long getaway every year to Malibu. The trip is seven days away. I want you to come with me."

"Oh, no. That's girlfriend territory."

He flails his hand about. "Don't flatter yourself. We just met, but ever since my divorce, my mother has been on me to date. She's old-fashioned and thinks I should be married with children by now.

"The thing is, I don't want a week alone with my family full of questions about why I'm still single. I want you to come and pretend to be my fiancé. After that, if you still want a no-strings relationship, then I'm all yours."

"Wait, what are you pitching here? I can't afford a trip to

Malibu. I'm hoping you're paying for this coffee," I joke, raising my cup.

"Quinn, I would pay for everything. All you'd have to do is show up. Anything you want."

My eyes flutter back up to meet his. "That bar of yours must do well if you can afford vacations to Malibu every year and to pay for my whole trip, too."

He makes a nonchalant motion with his head.

"I have a job, you know?" I remind him. "Some of us aren't the owners of our own successful businesses." Not to mention a child, but I don't tell him that.

He places his intertwined hands on the table and lowers his head.

I breathe in deeply and let out a louder than normal sigh. "Look, I'll see what I can do, okay? I'm not making any promises."

He grabs my hands in his and squeezes them. "Thank you, thank you, thank you."

He was right. I chose him for a reason. He's handsome and didn't seem to buy into the whole speed dating thing the others did. Truthfully, I could have gone for his friend, Phil, but I have a feeling Phil gets around. In today's world, choosing Phil would be like choosing which sexually transmitted disease I prefer.

Brett is different. I see something in him that mirrors me. I think he's been hurt, too, though he hides it well, and oddly, I want him even more now, knowing that he needs me as much as I need him. It's as if we were matched together in some cosmic way.

There's something beautiful about this arrangement. He helps me mend the broken pieces of my life, and I help him disguise his. I catch a glimpse of what it would be like to date him, but I push it from my mind, afraid I might fall in love with the idea.

"I think we should have some ground rules," I say.

He releases my hands. "Ground rules?"

"Yeah, for our relationship after Malibu... or rather lack thereof."

His eyes widen, and his lips purse together. "Okay. Shoot."

I'm not sure where to start, or even what the rules should be. There has to be something in place, though, to ensure we don't confuse sex for a relationship. "Um, okay, Rule Number One. The day after sex, we don't call one another."

He cocks his head. "Why?"

"Well, because that's something that always starts a relationship on the wrong foot. The girl expects the guy to call, and the guy never calls, and I don't want to be the girl that waits by the phone. I shouldn't be waiting for your call, and you shouldn't feel pressured to call."

He nods his head. "Okay, good rule. Got anymore?"

I'm sure I have a thousand, but I struggle to think of a couple more. "Okay, Rule Number Two. No spending the night at the other person's house. That's something either a couple would do or two drunk people end up doing after a one-night stand, and I don't want that awkward wake-up moment in my life right now."

"Well, that's going to be difficult," he says.

"Why?"

"Well, while we are on vacation, we will be sharing a room."

I think about this for a moment. "Okay, fair enough. But once we are home, the rule stands."

He seems confused. "What does that solve?"

"It solves the waking-up-after-falling-asleep-after-sex moment. Just humor me, okay?"

He throws his hands up as if surrendering. "Okay. You're the boss. Anything else?"

I'm sure there are more rules I'll think of as soon as I leave the coffee shop, but for the life of me, I can't think of any more. I'm just protecting myself. There must be limits. There has to be a line that can't be crossed.

I'm tired of being hurt, and the last time, when Spencer hurt me, it was bad. I've done a lot of soul-searching. I've had a husband. I don't need another. I have friends. I don't need any more.

Some people say you can never have too many friends, but that's not true. A lot of people equals a lot of chaos. I used to be a social butterfly. I would go out with the girls and had lots of friends. I've had my time as a young lady.

I'm past all that. I'm past wanting a lot of friends to keep up with. A lot of friends equal a lot of weddings, wedding showers, babies, and baby showers. That's not what I need in my life right now. I need an escape from life.

I need someone who is with me in the moment and who isn't thinking about what's to come, because he already knows there's nothing more to come. Someone who wants to have fun because he knows there's no pressure to make it official, call the next day, or work up to a proposal. Someone to be free with. For now, I think that person is Brett.

"No. Nothing else I can think of at the moment," I say.

He takes a gulp of coffee, and suddenly there's a large gap in the conversation. I bite my thumb nail nervously. What else is there to say?

"Tell me something," he says.

"What?" I ask quickly, happy that the conversation is moving forward.

"Who broke you?"

I'm taken aback. "Broke me?"

"I feel like I can ask you this, given our current situation."

"Who says I'm broken?" I'm torn between explaining myself and being insulted.

"Well, you have to admit not every woman would instigate a situation such as this."

"That doesn't mean I'm broken."

"Then what does it mean?" he asks.

I shrug. "Why does it have to mean anything? Why even question it? Isn't this like every man's fantasy?"

He stares down a moment. "No. Not every man." He then meets my eyes. My heart flutters.

"You know, if you can't handle this—" I begin.

He raises a hand to hush me. "There's nothing to handle. No strings attached. I get it, and I accept it. It's just something one of my employees said to me last night that has my head spinning a little."

I look him up and down. His posture is no longer straight but slumped as he twists his coffee cup in his hands. "What'd this person say?"

He lets out a sarcastic sound. "In not so many words? She said this is impossible."

"What is?"

He stares at me a moment. "A relationship without a relationship."

"Well, what do you think?" I'm not sure I want to know. I feel like he's either already backing out or getting too close. I don't want either, but I'm not sure which would be worse.

"I suppose only time will tell."

I feel a pain in the pit of my stomach. No, a knot. A knot twisting tighter and tighter. Here I am, unsure of myself again. Is it impossible?

"What else did she say?" My thumb now throbs from my gnawing.

"That's it. Of course, she could have just been saying that to get at me."

"Get at you?"

He grins. "She kind of has a crush on me."

"So, what's been the problem?"

He shakes his head. "She's just young. Impressionable. Her eyes are still young, only seeing what's on the outside."

"How young?" I ask as I feel my shoe brush against his under the table.

"Twenty-two."

"I can't believe I haven't thought to ask this yet, but how old are *you*?"

He laughs, and I join in. His laugh is rather contagious. "I'm thirty-five. You?"

"Thirty. Am I too young, too?"

We share a moment staring at one another. "No. You're not too young."

I tilt my head. "I'm not sure if that's a compliment or not."

I cover my mouth to hush further giggling. I have to remind myself that this isn't a date. This isn't my friend.

———

WE PART WAYS, and I find myself smiling into my scarf, but I quickly brush my hands over my face until it melts away. What am I doing?

When I arrive home, Evie jumps on me like she hasn't seen me in weeks. I smell her hair, and it brings me back to why I can't get into a relationship. I can't risk her being hurt again. I can't have her get attached to a man and the relationship not work out.

"So, how'd it go?" Fran asks from the kitchen.

"Fine. It went fine." I put Evie down and give her a pat on

the butt as she runs back to her room. Fran rounds the corner with two glasses of wine, and we both plop down on the sofa.

"So, what's he like?"

"It doesn't matter what he's like. He's a toy, Fran. Just a toy."

"Well isn't that just sex at its best!"

I slap her leg as she hands me a glass. "You realize it's ten in the morning and you're handing me wine."

"Yup!"

I chuckle, and she lays her head on my shoulder. "Seriously, what's he like?"

I sigh deeply. "He's... great, actually. He's got this laugh. There's a whole other world inside that laugh."

She lifts her head from my shoulder and turns to face me, setting her glass down in the process. "You haven't even slept with him yet, and you're already falling for him."

"I am *not* falling for him. All I said was he has a good laugh."

"Yeah, but that's how it always starts."

"With a laugh?"

"With loving something about them," she says, raising her brows at me.

"Nothing is starting. Well, there is one thing, though," I say with a bite of my bottom lip.

"Oh, no. What?"

"I'm going to Malibu with him in a week. That is, if I can get off work."

Her eyes widen, and her mouth drops. "What? How did we go from sex only to a romantic getaway?"

"It's not a romantic getaway. It's some vacation he's going on with his parents. He says we can't start our sex life until after I agree to come with him. So, I agreed."

"You're already meeting his parents?" she asks excitedly.

"Fran, it's not like that. It's just, well, he wants his mom off his back about dating or something, so I'm going to pretend to be his fiancé."

"Well, congratulations," she says raising her glass to mine.

"For what?"

"For the world's quickest engagement in modern-day history." Our glasses ting, and I roll my eyes as I take a larger than normal swig of red wine.

5

————

BRETT

I KNOW I've only known her for four days now, but I found myself sifting through excuses to see her today. As I put my wristwatch on and took note of my naked ring finger, an excuse came to me. I offered to meet her at her house, and she agreed, but it quickly led to Rule Number Three: no visiting one another's homes. She's getting stricter. Every time I take or even mention a step forward, she seems to push me two steps back.

I greet her with a cup of coffee at her door. "You know, people might say this is a date," she says.

"Which people would that be?"

"Um, every people. Picking me up at my home, coffee in tow, and taking me ring shopping."

"Well, we're supposed to be engaged for this trip. The illusion must be complete."

She shakes her head. "This is crazy."

"I agree. This whole thing is crazy."

"No, I mean, your family knows you, Brett. Apparently pretty well if you all go on yearly vacations together. Won't they be suspicious when you show up with some strange woman you claim to be engaged to?"

I shake my head. "No. Well, maybe." I laugh. "I'll tell my mother sometime soon, and trust me, it'll then spread through the family like wildfire."

"Oh, she's one of those," she says.

I give a knowing smile. "She's not a gossip. She just gets excited easily."

———

AS WE ARRIVE at the jewelry shop, we see a sea of wedding sets gleaming under the fluorescent lights. The diamonds glitter and shimmer, and purple and green twinkles ricochet off the glass showcases. Quinn's hands clutch the strap of the purse across her chest, as if she's afraid to touch anything. I put my arm around her and usher her to the first case.

"So, what kind of diamond do you want in your ring?"

She holds up a fist. "You see this?"

I tilt my head and laugh. "Yeah."

"Well, now you have an idea." She giggles. "I'm kidding. I don't see why you can't just get me a band. Why waste the money for the real deal?"

"Because my family knows I would never propose to a woman with just a band."

"Okay. Just don't make it too gaudy."

I laugh. "Every woman says that, and I've learned every woman's idea of gaudy is different."

We walk our separate ways for a while and scope out the sets. Soon, I see Quinn asking for assistance and pointing out a ring in a case. I walk behind her and glance over her shoulder as she tries on a simple solitaire ring with a heart for a diamond.

"Is that the one?" I ask.

She doesn't turn to meet my eyes. "My mother died of cancer some years back. I was pretty upset one day and tried not

37

to show it, but she could see. By then, she was living out of the hospital. She was bald from chemo, weak, and couldn't keep food down.

"One day, she took me by the hand and told me she knew I was scared, but she would always be with me. She told me, 'Every time you see a heart, it's me telling you I love you.'

"So now, every time I see one, I think of her, and it makes me feel a little safer, like it was planted there just for me, and that no matter what I've done in my life or where I've gone, I'm exactly where I'm supposed to be at that moment."

I turn her around, and there are tears in her eyes, but they don't fall. I raise her hand and admire the ring, twisting and turning it as it glitters against the lights. "I think we've found the one," I say.

She peers up into my eyes and simply nods.

We leave the store, and she's already wearing the ring. I know it's more for her mom's sake than mine, but she finally opened up to me a bit. I saw a softer side, not just a crazy lady with a crazy idea.

The moment in the jewelry store reminded me that I know little about her. I didn't know her mother had died. What about her father? Does she have other siblings?

"Tell me about yourself," I urge.

She glances in my direction and then right back down to the sidewalk as we stroll the streets back to her condo. "What do you want to know?"

I shrug. "Anything. We have to know things about each other if we plan to play as though we're engaged. Is your father still around?"

"We didn't have a father for long. He left when we were young. From what I hear, he made himself a new family elsewhere."

"That's terrible."

"That's men," she says.

I jerk my head back. "That's men?"

"Well, all I've ever known of them."

It's coming together now. "So, your husband..."

"Found a woman elsewhere."

I finally stare down at my feet as we walk, just as she does. "I'm sorry." She ignores my apology.

"What about you?"

"Yeah, I was married before, too."

"She find someone new?"

I chuckle. "May the Lord be with the poor soul if she did."

"That bad, huh?"

"Worse."

It's quiet as we come up on her place. "You want to come inside?" she asks. "Have a glass of wine?"

"I thought you said no visiting one another's houses."

"I did. After today." I know what she wants. But she can't have it. Not yet.

I politely make my goodbyes and leave.

————

"SO, uh, how'd it go with Quinn today?" Phil asks.

I close my eyes and shake my head. "It went perfectly fine."

"You humped her, didn't you?" he jokes, plopping down on my couch with a beer.

"Humped? Classy, Phil. But no, I didn't."

"Hey, when you decided to arrange sex with a complete stranger right in front of me, it ceased to become a private matter. So, spill."

I untuck my shirt from my jeans. "I happened to have an intimate moment with her, but it did not lead to sex.

"Intimate?"

39

"Yeah, she kind of opened up to me today."

"Hmm. Well, whatever."

I chuckle. "Were you born with no filter, or is this just something that built up over time?"

"C'mon, c'mon. Stop procrastinating. Tell me what she's like"

"She was great," I finally admit. "There's much more she has to offer than just sex."

"What do you mean? There's more between you than sex? You a couple now?"

"No. No. I mean there's more to her than that. If it weren't for all her rules, she'd be the kind of person I'd actually date. That being said, she *is* going to meet my family."

He slams the beer down on the table. "She's going to Malibu with you? Brett, I have to go, and you have to talk her into bringing her friend."

"What? What are you talking about? You don't even like Fran. You just can't stand that she doesn't like *you*." Phil has been aching all these years to go to Malibu with us, but the fact that he has no filter terrifies me for my mother's sake. It would be just like him to bring up sex at the dinner table or something.

Perhaps, though, if Fran did come along, it would keep him occupied. Plus, I'm sure Quinn would feel more comfortable. I hated to ask her to come with me because I know meeting someone's parents puts a lot of pressure on a person. Especially in our situation. But I didn't hate it enough not to ask.

If she's going to use me for what she needs and wants, I don't see anything wrong with doing the same. Apparently, she doesn't either, because as we speak, she has agreed.

"Brett, I don't ask you for much..."

"You're joking, right?" I laugh. He asks me for things daily.

"Just ask, Brett! I know you can afford to bring us all."

"Now you're asking me to pay your way, and not just your way but Fran's way, too. You don't ask for much?"

"C'mon, trust fund baby," he laughs.

I roll my eyes. I hate it when he calls me that. I picture a trust fund baby as a person who doesn't work for a living, but the truth is, my trust fund bought me the bar, and he, being my best friend, knows that.

"I'll see what I can do," I say.

"Yes!"

"Hey! I make no promises."

6

QUINN

I WOKE up no longer doubting myself or my decision to be so forward with him. There was a freedom in living in the moment and having no other objective than to please myself. No promises of calls and waiting by the phone. No working toward something that may or may not happen, like a relationship or proposal.

No false hope. No empty words. No promises. Just a release from everything around us for a short period of time. Nothing else mattered.

I've never felt so exhilarated before. Even with his absurd condition looming over my head, I've never been so in charge of a situation, or even my life. I'm going to enjoy this, and if a week in Malibu, all expenses paid, is the price I have to pay to keep this in my life, well, I guess I'll make the sacrifice.

"Hey," I say answering the door to Spencer and Evie.

"Hey, I got to run. Melissa is waiting in the car." Melissa, the woman, or girl I should say, that stole my husband from me. Just hearing her name makes me want to punch him in the jaw.

"Well, we need to talk."

"About what?"

"I'm going to need you to keep Evie next week. I'm going out of town. I'm taking a small vacation."

He jerks his head back. "With who?"

My eyes narrow at him. "That's not any of your business. You can do this for me. She's your daughter, too."

He flutters his eyelids as if annoyed. "What day do I need to pick her up?"

"I'm not sure yet. I'll let you know soon."

"Fine," he says with a wave of his hand as he walks off.

I close the door and lean against it. I hate that I still love and think about him. I wish more than anything that I could have a decent relationship with him and be one of those open-minded women who accept what has happened to them and befriend the "other woman."

But I can't see myself doing that right now. Even though I have my own things going on at the moment, and I'm happy; I just can't. It's still too soon. Every time I see his face, every time I hear her name, there's a pain in my chest and a wrenching sensation in my gut.

There's a knock on the door, and Fran peeks her head in. "Knock, knock!"

"Come on in, girl."

"Passed Spencer on the way in."

"Lucky you," I mutter.

"Why are there wine glasses on the table?" she asks, picking them up to take to the kitchen.

"Well, they were left over from you and me. Don't get any ideas. He turned me down when I invited him in."

"Well, inviting him to your house... where you live... where Evie lives... think that's smart? You've only known the guy for five days."

"It's not going to happen again. I've made rules."

"Oh, this I got to hear," she laughs.

43

"It's not as stupid as you might think. No call backs the day after sex, no visiting one another's houses, and no spending the night with one another."

"Ha! You think that's going to keep you from falling for him? Besides, you haven't spent a romantic trip with him... yet."

My head snaps her way, as she peers at me through the kitchen opening. "I'm not going to fall for him."

"Quinn, what's this kick you're on all of a sudden?"

"It's called getting divorced and having your priorities change. I'm not falling for him."

"Come on, Quinn. He's in your age bracket, owns his own business, and takes yearly trips to the beach. Geez, *I* want to fall in love with him," she says, sitting on the couch with a clean wine glass filled to the rim.

I'm a realist. I know how easy it would be to fall in love with someone like Brett, but I can't think about him in a romantic way. I can't think of anyone that way. Not yet. Which is why I made the rules in the first place.

It wasn't to keep him away. It was to keep me away. To remind me that my only concern right now is fixing *me*.

———

TODAY I SEE BRETT AGAIN. This time he called me, which is surprising. I thought it would take a lot longer for him to feel comfortable enough to initiate things. It's technically been less than a week, after all. He rented a nice hotel room, just for the day. Or rather the end of the day. I shuffle home from work, jump in the shower, shave, and I'm off to meet him.

I'm torn between feeling sleazy and feeling invigorated. Maybe he's come to his senses. If we can't meet at one another's houses, though, I suppose I left him no choice. I'm shocked, however, that when I arrive at the room, he just wants to talk.

44

"So, I have a question."

"You rented a hotel room to question me?"

"We can't meet at each other's work or house, so what choice did I have for privacy?"

I roll my eyes, knowing he's right again. "What is it?"

"Do you want to bring Fran with you to Malibu? I thought it might make you a little more comfortable to have a friend there."

"Yeah, I'll have to ask her. It might be a little difficult for both of us to go, though," I admit.

"Why's that?"

"Because we work together. I'm not sure we can both be gone at the same time."

"Wow, I didn't know you worked together. Actually, come to think of it, I don't even know what you do for a living," he admits.

"I'm a high school coach. Fran is the assistant coach."

"I would have never guessed that. You don't seem the sort."

I smile, but it doesn't reach my eyes. "How would you know? You barely know me."

"True. I guess I just always pictured women coaches as more... rough."

"Rough?"

"Yeah, rough around the edges. Not as beautiful and as ladylike."

I tilt my head. "Ladylike. After all of this, you think I'm ladylike. I'm not sure whether I'm appreciative or amused."

He laughs. "You can be both. So, what do you coach?"

"Girls' fast-pitch softball."

His eyebrows lift as he fiddles with a button on his shirt. "Impressive."

For some reason, I don't like discussing myself with him. I'm not ready to let anyone *in* just yet, much less a man I basically picked up off the street. I quickly change the subject back to him. If there's one thing I've learned, men love talking about themselves just as much, if not more, than women. Honestly, I think most men are just in love with the sound of their own voices.

"What about you? How long have you owned your bar?"

"Hmm. Well, let's see now. Three years."

"That's pretty striking. They say most small businesses don't last past two years."

"I got lucky is all."

"How so?"

"I know a lot of drunks," he says.

I can't help but giggle, and somehow that small laugh allows me to calm down a little bit and relax.

"So, what's the real reason you want Fran to come to Malibu?"

He sighs. "Phil wants to come. He asked if I would entice you to bring Fran."

I laugh. "He knows Fran can't stand him."

"Yeah, he knows, but he can't stand that Fran can't stand him," he chuckles.

"What's Phil's deal? Does he like Fran? Or is he just one of those guys who wants to be wanted?"

"You know, I don't know. Honestly, I think he's fascinated by her. It's not often a woman turns him down. I hear he's quite the charmer."

"And probably heartbreaker," I spit out. I know his kind. His kind is the reason Rule Number One is in play. Had Fran bought into his nonsense that first night and gone home with him, there would have been nothing but skid marks and silence the next day, and Fran probably saw that train wreck coming.

"He's broken some hearts. Haven't we all though?"

I purse my lips and shake my head. "You may be a heartbreaker, but I've never had the opportunity. Guys always seem to beat me to the punch."

He stares at me for a second and shoves his hands in his pockets. "So, that's it then?"

"What's it?"

"That's the reason for all the rules and only wanting sex. You want a man in your life, but you don't want to give him the opportunity to hurt you."

I sit on the edge of the bed, not wanting to meet his dark eyes. I'm afraid if he sees my eyes, he'll know he's right. If I could wiggle my nose and be out of this room without his even seeing me, I would. "I've told you before. I've played the game and don't care to again."

"Not every man is playing a game, Quinn."

"I know that." I say it, and I mean it. I know there are some guys out there who are ready to settle down and who are capable of being loyal, but I can't see that far ahead right now. I can't see that at all yet.

"This time, you're the one playing the game, Quinn. Making up the rules as you go along."

"You agreed to the game, and you agreed to the rules," I remind him almost angrily.

He nods. "Yeah, I did."

I finally meet his eyes. There's a knowledge in them. Like he knows me better than I know myself now.

"You're broken," he says.

I shake my head. "No, I *was* broken. Now I'm being maintained."

I stand up and head for the door. I place my hand on the door knob and leave quickly before he can respond.

———

"HE'S GOT to be rich. You think he's one of those trust fund babies?" Fran asks as she gobbles down leftover pasta from a container in my fridge.

"Probably. I don't know any other guy our age who can afford to pay for four people to go to Malibu, all expenses paid."

I hear the fridge slam closed, and she walks into the living room with her brows pushed together. "What do you mean four people? Who else is he paying for besides us? Please don't tell me..."

"Yes, his friend, Phil."

"Oh, no. I'm not going."

"Fran, you have to do this for me. Come on. You said yourself—this guy could be a psycho, and I'll be hundreds of miles away with him."

She shakes her head as she takes another large bite. "That's your problem now. You're a big girl."

I lean my head back on the couch and tilt it onto her shoulder and sniffle.

"Don't. Don't do that fake crying thing. That's pitiful. I'll tell you what, if he agrees to fly us first class, I'll go. I need something first class in my life right now. By the way, this pasta sucks," she says, taking another large bite. "When are you going to talk to him again?"

"Not sure, but I'll let him know."

We sit in silence for a while, sipping our wine with the television muted on the evening news.

"I still say this is no way to live," Fran says.

"I'm not living."

She sits up and turns to me, placing her glass on the table and taking my glass and doing the same. She takes my hands. "What *are* you doing then?"

I lower my head. "Having fun," I mutter.

She shakes her head. "You don't look like you're having fun to me, Quinn."

My eyes fall away. "I don't know what I'm doing. Sometimes I think I'm having fun. Sometimes I think I'm crazy, and this is the dumbest thing I've ever done."

"You know what I think?"

I smile slightly, knowing she will tell me regardless. "What do you think?"

"I think Brett is a good guy. A guy with his own business, goals, friends, and family. I think you two are a lot alike. He could be the answer for you, and you're throwing it away because you're choosing to use him, in your mind, before he uses you."

"There was a time I thought Spencer was the answer for me, too."

"You can't compare every man you meet to Spencer."

"I'm just afraid if it happened again, it would hurt so bad I'd just shrivel up and never be able to love anyone else."

She shakes her head as she stares into my eyes. "No one said loving someone is easy, but spending your life avoiding love is lonely."

7

BRETT

"I DON'T UNDERSTAND, dear. How can you be engaged when we haven't even met her? We didn't even know you were seeing anyone."

I know this should seem easy, but in all honesty, it's actually difficult to lie to my mother. Still, letting her find out I haven't seen anyone since Lisa would be much, much more lecture-worthy. I've been seeing Quinn a week now. That's got to count for something, right?

"Well, Mom, you know I'm a private person."

"I know, dear, but, well, what's she like? How'd you meet her?"

Do I say speed dating? She probably wouldn't care how we met, but telling my mother we met at speed dating just sounds too cheesy, even for her.

"Phil introduced us," I lie.

"Oh, honey. Not Phil." Yeah, I probably should have come up with a better answer. Better yet, I probably should have planned this conversation before I called her. She likes Phil, but she's also seen the kind of women Phil has brought around.

"Yeah, Mother. She's a nice woman. She's beautiful, smart,

and energetic. She works with high school students." Finally, a truthful answer.

"Well, she sounds lovely, Brett. I'm anxious to meet her. I'm sure your father and sister will be, too."

"She can't wait to meet you all either." I'm sure another lie. "So, do you think it's okay with the family if she and her friend join us in Malibu this week?"

"Well, of course, dear," she says. "She's going to be your wife, after all."

With that, it finally dawns on me the position I've put myself in. If my mother meets Quinn and falls in love with her, how will I explain that we aren't together anymore after we get back from the trip?

Do I say we broke up? I'm sure my mother would ask *why* we broke up. What would I tell her then? This seemed like a good idea at the time, but now I'm not so sure.

Do I just pray that my mother ends up disapproving of her? Seems like a terrible thing to wish for, but I've already dedicated myself to this idea. There's nothing left to do than follow through with this madness.

———

SELLING Quinn to my mother was a piece of cake. The real challenge will be selling her to my sister, Anne. She's my twin sister, and we can always see through one another's lies as if we share the same mind. I wish I could just call her and feed her the lies, but I'm already supposed to meet her and my niece, Nell, at the park.

I suppose I could tell Anne the truth, but I can't put that on her shoulders. She would be lying to our parents and her daughter, too. That wouldn't be right. I'm going to have to dig deep to be convincing. It's times like this that I wish I knew more about Quinn. Maybe I'd be able to be more convincing if I did.

I arrive at the park and see my sister sitting at a wooden picnic table, watching Nell on the swing set. I suck in a breath and walk her way.

"Hi, Uncle Brett!" Nell hollers from her swing.

I wave to her as I take a seat next to Anne.

"Mom just called me," she says tapping her phone. I already know before she says anything else that Mom has beaten me to the punch. "Since when do you trust Phil to fix you up with women?"

"What can I say? He's constantly trying to fix me up, and I finally gave in one night. It's a good thing I did," I lie.

She shakes her head. "This whole situation is fishy. Since when don't you tell me about your relationships?"

"Since the last one crashed and burned. I didn't want to say anything until I knew for sure she was the one. You all already had to deal with me during my divorce. I didn't want you getting attached to someone who might not be around for long."

I can't believe how convincing I sound. Even I'm starting to believe it. She looks away from me to check on Nell, and I glance with her. I even hate lying to my niece. What if Nell gets attached to her, too? I hadn't thought of that.

"So, what's she like?" she asks.

I raise my eyebrows. I can tell the truth now, I think. "She's a softball coach at a high school, intelligent, adventurous, and she keeps me on my toes. She has a big heart. I think she's been hurt before, even more so than I, but she's a good person, if a little misunderstood."

Everything I said is true in my eyes. I think other people might take her brassiness the wrong way at times, but I can see past it. I can see myself in her. It could have been just as easy for me to look at the world differently, especially women.

"What's she look like?" she asks.

"Oh, well, she's gorgeous. She has dark hair, average height, I suppose, green eyes. She's beautiful."

She purses her lips together slightly. "Brains and beauty, huh? Sounds too good to be true."

"Oh, she has her faults, I assure you," I say and mean it.

"Like what?"

I shake my head. "When we first met, she had some trust issues, but we've worked those out."

"What do you mean? She thought you were cheating?"

"No, no. Nothing like that, just afraid I would break her heart. In the beginning, she refused to get too close." I know I'm lying, but in a sense, I'm telling the truth. I'm just speaking as if she has moved past her faults when she hasn't.

"Why do you think that is?"

"Well, she's divorced. Her ex had an affair. I don't think it ended on good terms, but she doesn't talk about it."

Anne nods her head slightly and stares into my eyes, as if she's waiting on me to slip up and say something wrong. "You coming to the family dinner tonight? I'm sure Dad would love to hear all about your new fiancé."

I stare back at her for a moment. "Yeah. Yeah, I'll be there."

———

I WALK through the streets of Manhattan on my way home. I watch my feet as I walk, wishing there were dirt or even pebbles to kick around. I've gotten myself into a terrible spot.

"Fancy meeting you here," a familiar voice says.

I glance up. "Quinn?"

She chuckles. "Where are you headed?"

I glance around with my hands in my pockets nervously.

"You know, I don't know. I just have some time to kill before tonight. Just walking the streets."

She nods. "Me, too. So, what happens tonight?"

I suck in a deep breath. "Dinner with my family. I told them about you this morning."

"Oh, and...?"

I tilt my head slightly. "It went as expected, I suppose."

She leans her head in to stare in my eyes. "Something's wrong."

I shake my head. "I don't enjoy lying to my family."

She scoffs. "I've never met a man who had trouble with lying."

Her thoughts of men are getting exceedingly more annoying. "Not all men are out to hurt you, Quinn. Or anyone for that matter."

"I know that."

I shake my head. "I don't think you do. You speak of men as if they all have the same agenda. If I thought that way about women after my divorce, I would have to assume you're a money grubbing..." My voice trails off and I take a deep breath. Her head lowers and I spit out a "never mind" before I head to walk past her.

"Wait," she says.

"What?"

"Just... wait. I'm sorry. You're right."

I stare back to her.

"Where is it you're going tonight? I want to come with you," she says.

I laugh through my nose sarcastically. "Trust me, you don't."

"Just tell me where."

I tilt my head up to the sky and rub my eyes before I peek back at her. "My parents' house. They want to know about you."

She breathes deeply. "I'll come with you."

"You're joking, right?"

"I can be quite charming when I want to be. I can help you."

As much as I hate to admit it, I could use her assistance, and she's being honest when she says she knows how to be charming. I've seen it.

Although, her calling out to me today and now offering to go with me is a bit confusing. She has my head all scrambled. I told my sister she keeps me on my toes, and that she does. I never know which side of her I'm going to get. Today, I got a little of both.

"Okay. You can come."

She nods. "Okay."

———

WE WALK the streets for another hour, learning little things about one another, and for the first time, I have her truly laughing. I tell her all about my family and what she can expect from them — basically a million and one questions — and when dinner rolls around, she is the most charming woman in the world. She makes my family laugh and shoots silly faces to Nell to make her giggle.

It's a side of her I've never seen. I catch myself staring at her and taking in little details I haven't noticed before, like the fullness of her lips when she smiles, the way the light glints off her crystal earrings dangling from her dainty ears, the diamond heart ring she is wearing on her hand, and the red tint to her brown hair when the light hits it just right.

My family eats it up. Every morsel. It's been a long time since my family has seemed so cheerful, but for a moment I catch myself feeling sad in the midst of the happy affair.

This is all fake. It isn't real. It isn't mine, but I'm not allowed to think like that, so I laugh with the rest of them.

———

"SO, HOW'D I DO?" she asks as I walk her home.

"Charming as ever. I was a fool for ever doubting you."

"You doubted me?" she laughs, shoving me with her shoulder.

"I won't make the mistake again."

Silence falls for a moment. "You still seem sad."

I shake my head. "Are you ready for the trip now that you've met everyone?" Yes, I'm avoiding her question.

"I feel a little more comfortable now, yeah." Well, that makes one of us. "What about you?"

"Honestly, I'm just glad you convinced everyone. My mother is a worrier, and Anne is a suspicious soul."

"What about your dad?"

"I don't worry so much about my dad. He's the quiet type. A man of few words."

Once we arrive at her place, I start to sweat even though it's fall. I don't want her to ask me to come inside tonight. I couldn't turn her down after what she did for me today, but obviously, I'm not in the mood. I have too much on my mind.

She glances up.. "Well, thanks for walking me home, as always. You're a real gentleman."

My head cocks. "Are you sure you think so?"

Her face drops slightly, but she takes a step toward me. I wait for her to take my hand from my pocket or pull me into a kiss, something to initiate sex, but with one more step toward me, she brushes her face against mine for only a moment and kisses me gently on my cheek. "I'm sure."

She then turns toward her building and walks away, giving

me a single wave goodbye. I stand there, statuesque, for a moment. What has she done to me?

She has taken my brain and twisted it like putty in her hands. One minute she's pushing for sex, and the next she's offering to help me convince my parents we're engaged. She plays both parts so well that even I can't decipher truth from fiction—if there is any truth.

8

QUINN

WHEN I ARRIVE home from Brett's parent's house, Thomas and Fran are already at my place, ready to ambush me with questions. I should have known better than to give them keys. They know I was with Brett, and now I'm unsure whether to lie about having a good time or not. If I tell them I had a pleasant evening with him, without sex, they are sure to think we have a dating situation.

"So, tell us everything," Fran says as I set my purse down on the table.

I shake my head slightly. "Don't you two have home lives?"

They stare at each other. "Is this not our home?" Thomas jokes. "I could have sworn I lived here."

"Well, now that you mention it..." I joke back.

"Hey, I'm the babysitter. I'm supposed to be here," Fran boasts.

I take the scarf from around my neck and fling it over the arm chair. "Where's Evie?"

"She's in her room," says Thomas.

"I see Prince Charming walked you to your door again. I

didn't even know you were going out with him tonight," Fran says.

"I didn't either, actually," I reply.

"He picks you up at your door, he buys you jewelry, you meet at coffee shops, and he walks you to your door. You're dating," Thomas says.

I chuckle. "We're both holding up our ends of the bargain. He wanted me to convince his parents tonight that we're a couple. It's all part of the sham. Relax."

"Get real," Fran chimes in. "You could have told him no and moved on to the next guy."

"Yeah, and the next guy might have wanted something in return," I say.

"All guys want something in return," says Thomas. "Just like all women."

"Exactly," I say.

I peek into Evie's bedroom and see her watching a movie on her TV. I smile, and shut her door quietly before returning to the living area.

"So, what are his folks like?" Fran asks.

I shrug. "Like anyone else's folks."

"Did you like them?"

"Sure, I liked them. I think you'll like them, too."

"When is Fran going to meet them?" Thomas asks.

"You didn't tell him?" I ask Fran.

Her eyes widen. "I forgot."

"Fran has been invited to Malibu with us. Brett thought it might make me feel more comfortable."

"Well, isn't that thoughtful of him?" Thomas sarcastically breathes out before plopping back down on the sofa with a glass of wine.

"I have to run. We have an early scrimmage with the girls

tomorrow, and I have to start packing for the trip. You should, too."

I nod to her, and as she leaves, I get a sinking feeling in my stomach. It's as if my only ally is leaving. Something about Thomas's last remark has me worried. Thomas has a tendency to be unpredictable. Sometimes he's perfectly fine with me, and other times it's as if everything I say or do annoys him. We've had our share of heated discussions, especially over Spencer.

I pour myself a glass of wine, although I had plenty at dinner, and sit at the end of the sofa closest to him. "What's on your mind, Thomas?"

He takes a sip of wine and shakes his head. "Do you even think about the things you do before you do them?"

"What are you talking about?"

"Like offering a stranger sex or accepting a paid vacation with a stranger. Perhaps accepting gifts like the ring. You're not just a sex toy to this guy, Quinn."

"What do you mean?"

"I mean, you see him almost every day. I know you, and I know how easy you fall, and from a guy's point of view, trust me, he has already fallen."

"So, what are you saying? I should call off the trip?" What does it even matter to him? Why does this upset him so much?

"I'm not here to tell you what to do. I'm here to tell you what you *are* doing and let you decide what your next step is. If you want this guy, then go on your trip, but if you don't want a relationship and aren't interested in him, then leave him be before one or both of you get hurt."

"Why do you care so much if I hurt this guy?"

His chest rises as he breathes in, and I see his jaw clench. "Because I know what it's like to love a woman who doesn't love you back."

My head jerks back. I've never known Thomas to be in love. "Who do you love?"

He finally turns his head and looks me in the eye slowly. His expression melts, and it all finally becomes clear. Now I know why we always fought. I know why he hated Spencer so much for hurting me. I know why he doesn't want me to hurt Brett.

I shake my head. "Why have you never told me?"

He sarcastically chuckles. "When would I have told you?"

"You could have told me at any time."

"When? When you were married to Spencer? During your divorce? Or now, when apparently all you want is sex?"

———

BY THE TIME THOMAS LEFT, all our cards were on the table. He knows I love him, but not in the same way he loves me. Honestly, I have never thought of him romantically before, and I can't think of him romantically now.

I can no longer honestly say that all I want right now is sex. It's only that I want some sort of relationship with no expectations. Expectations get people hurt, and that's what I would have to deal with if I gave Thomas another thought right now. I'll think about him later.

The truth is, tonight I'm not thinking of Thomas anymore. Tonight opened a door for me. Even though I know I was only playing a role with Brett's folks, it gave me a sense of what it would feel like to be carefree again. Some would think it would feel more like a commitment, but having a family again seemed to come so natural to me. I do miss having family get-togethers.

I tuck Evie into bed with a short goodnight story and a kiss on her forehead and shut her door, leaving it cracked just a touch as she likes it. I pick up the phone and dial Spencer's number with a newfound sense of purpose. It rings only once.

"Hello?" Spencer says.

"Spencer."

"Quinn? It's late. What's going on?"

"Yeah, I know. I just wanted to tell you that I thought about it, and Melissa taking Evie to the movies is okay with me."

There's a long pause. "Thank you, Quinn."

"Yeah, no problem."

"Quinn."

"Yes?"

"We, uh, never got to talk after... well, after you found out about Melissa. She's gone out with a friend tonight. I'd like to come talk to you if I can. Shell some things out. Maybe put some things behind us."

Now there's a long pause on my end. There are so many questions I had wanted answered from him that he refused to give me at the time. Now I'm not so sure I want the answers. I recall thinking the other day that I wished we were on better terms, so I agree to his coming over for a few minutes while Evie sleeps.

I'm not sure why I agreed to let Melissa go alone with my child. Maybe so I'm not postponing the inevitable anymore. I'd like to say I don't have a problem with Melissa personally, but I can't help but feel disgusted when I think of a woman so carelessly having sex with a married man who has a family. Melissa is too young to realize that if he will do it to me, then he will do it to her.

When I say young, I mean she is only twenty-one. Spencer, on the other hand, is thirty-seven. I chuckle to myself at the thought of Melissa taking Evie to see a movie. It's probably because they both still enjoy cartoons.

"Spencer," I say, answering the door a half hour later. "Would you like a glass of wine or a beer maybe?"

"A beer would be great, thanks."

I nod and close the door behind him before heading off to the kitchen where I can roll my eyes at my own stupidity for having him over here. What was I thinking? This is so awkward.

I refill my wine glass before heading back into the living room and handing him a beer.

"Thanks," he mutters.

"So, what's on your mind?"

He laughs nervously. "I'm not real sure. I wasn't expecting your call tonight, and you caught me at a weak moment."

"What do you mean?"

He puts the untouched beer on the table. "I saw you at the coffee shop the other day with some guy."

I raise my brows. "Okay?"

He shrugs. "It just got me thinking about what could have been had I not screwed everything up."

I'm astounded. This is the first time he has admitted that he broke our family apart. Before this, he acted like all his actions were somehow justified.

"It would have never worked out between us," I say.

His head jerks back. "Why?"

"Because if it wasn't with Melissa, it would have been with someone else. I never made you happy. It didn't matter what I did."

"That's not true. You always made me happy. I'm the one who couldn't make myself happy. I thought it was you, but it wasn't. It was my problem all along."

I shake my head. "Where's all this coming from?"

He licks his lips and lowers his head. "I'm just... so sorry that I hurt you. I'm so sorry about what I did. I want to make it right."

"Spencer, there's no way to make what you did right." He lowers his head further. "Look, what's done is done and in the past. I've moved on with my life. The guy you saw at the coffee shop is only a friend."

"Is he?"

"Does it matter?"

"I suppose not."

I nod. "All we can do is make sure we take care of Evie now. I fought my own battles about Melissa, but the truth is, if Melissa is a decent person and she cares about Evie, then I just see her as one more person who can love, look after, and take care of my child."

"Is it that easy? Do you truly see it that way?"

"*Easy?* Nothing these past six months has been easy, but that's the only way I can look at things without losing my mind. No, it's not easy. You've made everything difficult for me for years, and it affects my relationships even today.

"I don't look at men like I used to. Friends treat me differently. I have serious trust issues. I can admit to all of that, and yes, that's partially your fault, but I can't live my life being angry anymore. You made your choices, and I made mine. Our only focus now should be co-parenting our daughter."

He sits up slightly in his chair and picks up his beer, opening it and taking a single drink before placing it back down. "Quinn, I still love you."

I stare into his eyes. I believe that he *thinks* he still loves me, but a man who cheats on his wife no longer has a concept of love, in my opinion. "That's your misfortune."

"Can you sit there and honestly say you don't love me anymore?" he asks.

I take a few seconds to consider his question. I think of the differences between him and Brett. Brett allows me to at least make half of the rules. He doesn't push me away, and he doesn't pull me toward him. He lets me come and go as I please.

I even consider the difference between him and Thomas.

Thomas loved me so much that for years he couldn't burden me with the truth of his love for me. Even though he apparently has loved me since we were young.

"I'll always care for you, Spencer. You're the father of my child. You've been in my life since I was seventeen. You practically raised me from a teenager, but, no, I'm not in love with you anymore."

He stares down at his beer, taking one last sip. He places it firmly on the table and pushes off his knees to a standing position. "I'm glad we had this talk," he says. "Can I hug you goodbye?"

"Of course."

We share a hug, and I let him out the door, proud of everything I learned about myself today.

9

BRETT

"YOU LOOK AWFULLY FAMILIAR," I say as I open the door to Quinn, "but you can't be who I think you are because that would mean you were breaking one of your own rules." It was her idea not to visit one another's homes, yet here she is, standing in the hall of my apartment building.

"Oh, hush and get me a drink," she says, pushing past me and walking right in.

"Well, won't you come in?" I joke.

"Sorry, I just had a long night."

"Beer okay?"

"That's fine."

"You know, some might say we are dating," I remark, walking to the kitchen and popping the cap off a beer.

"Some already do."

I already know who before I ask. "Who says that? Your friend, Fran?"

"Not just her, but yes."

A small part of me loves the idea. It would be so easy for me to fall in love with Quinn, despite her obvious trust issues. Yes, I can see us falling for one another in time. "So, why are you here?"

She takes a large drink of her beer. Her eyes dart around my apartment. Her body is tense, and she looks like she could cry at any moment. "Because I have no place else to go."

"I'm sure that's not true," I tell her, taking an equally large gulp.

"No, I mean, I have other places to go tonight, it's just that last night, my whole life seemed to come to a head, and I needed an escape."

I take a chance and pull her close to me, finally allowing myself to kiss her. Her breath on my lips is everything right now.

"This feels different with you," she says into my lips, her breath on my mouth.

"Is that wrong?" I ask, breathing heavily. She shakes her head and kisses me harder.

But I can tell if I don't stop it here, it will go farther. So I take a step back. "Stop. You know the rules. The first one being no sex, yet. The second being no sex at one another's house." I'm getting more impatient with her. "You're making up the rules as you go along and breaking them just as fast. Do *you* even know what you want?"

She raises her chin. "I just want to feel something."

"Why? So you can run away from it the second it ends?" She drops her hands to her side. "Just stick to the rules, Quinn. I'm not going to be something else you have to survive. Just... stay a while and behave."

"Then what should we do?"

"It doesn't matter. We can be friends, too. We'll order Chinese and watch television like friends do."

"Do you truly think we can do that? Be friends?

"Do you honestly think you can keep going the way you are without complicating things?" I ask.

She sits on the edge of the couch and rubs her head. I don't know what to do with her anymore. I don't know what I'm allowed to feel or say or think. My brain is scrambled eggs, and my ego is long gone.

"What Chinese restaurant do you like?" she asks.

A small victory.

———

"SO, how did you find out where I live anyway?" I ask, taking a large, earned bite of dumpling.

She swallows a bite herself. "Wasn't hard. I went to your bar. Phil was there, and he told me."

"Oh. I'm sure I'll be hearing about that later."

She chuckles. "Your friends must be as nosey as mine."

"I can assure you they're worse."

"There was a girl there giving me ugly looks."

I nod my head. "That would be Janine."

"Oh, sorry. I guess my coming in there to ask where you live isn't going to help that situation."

"Probably not. It's okay. She knows about you. As do the others, thanks to Phil."

She eats her food hungrily as we watch a flick, but seriously, I don't even know the name of it. I'm only concentrated on stealing glimpses of her when she's not paying attention to me.

She's so different from my ex-wife, Lisa. Lisa is beautiful: thin with long red hair and always fashionable. I was immediately attracted to her, but the way she looked was a sad trap. As beautiful as she is on the outside, she is cold as ice on the inside.

There was a blackness in her eyes at times, as if there were no soul there. She would turn heads wherever we went. The perfect arm candy, but not wife material. Unfortunately, I didn't know that until she *was* my wife.

Quinn is much different. She doesn't have a perfect body. Some might even say she's rather ordinary in appearance, but to me, she's beautiful. I could make a list of reasons why Quinn is a better match for me than Lisa ever was.

She places a box of half-eaten noodles down and sits with her legs crossed in the chair, brushing her hands off, although they are clean. "We better get some particulars about one another before we spend a whole week with your family."

"Okay," I say, "like what?"

"Well, to be quite honest, I was so nervous the other night that I can't remember your parents' names. I know your sister is Anne and her daughter is Nell."

"If you were nervous, you didn't show it, but my mother's name is Kathryn and my father is Joe."

"That's right. That's right," she mutters to herself.

"And your brother is Randy, who plays the drums." Then it dawns on me that I could have told my mother that's how Quinn and I met. Through her brother who plays at my bar. It surely would have been a better way than saying we met through Phil. What's done is done.

"What was your mother's name?" I ask her.

She smiles and stares down. "Her name was Dorothy. She had fire-red hair and always wore red lipstick."

I know now how she got the red tint in her hair. Her smile as she talks about her mother is all I need to know about the kind of relationship they had.

"Is asking about your father a sore subject?"

She shrugs. "He left when I was eight. Randy was six. I have good memories of us. At the time, I didn't understand why he left. It wasn't until I was older that mother told us he had fallen in love with another woman."

"I'm sorry." How could a man have done this to his children? I can't imagine a man picking up and leaving his babies behind for another woman. I understand divorce and always will, but not a grown man leaving his children behind...

"I suppose I was doomed to walk in my mother's footsteps. Once I was a teenager, I tried to look him up but could never find anything on him. I guess he didn't want us to." She paused. "I have a question," she says, scooting up in her seat.

"Shoot."

She chuckles lightly. "What is your last name?"

I laugh loudly, and she follows suit. "Yeah, that's probably need-to-know information."

"Yes!"

"My last name is Redding. What about you?"

"Kennedy."

"Wow. I feel like I should bow or something."

She giggles. "Well, go ahead."

"Any relation?"

"Afraid not," she laughs. "So, what about your sister? Is she married?"

I nod and pick up Quinn's box of noodles. "Yeah, she's married. His name is Russell, but everyone calls him Russ. He'll be going on the trip with us, too."

"Wow. A lot of people are going on this trip," she says nervously.

"It's okay, Quinn. That just means there's a lot of distractions there."

Her grin returns. "So, tell me about your ex-wife. What happened there? If I'm crossing a line, just tell me."

I shake my head. "You're not. She was perfect at first, but as soon as we said, 'I do' she changed."

"How so?"

"She became obsessed with money, but she didn't want to work. Which, don't get me wrong, I don't mind taking care of my wife, but she had us up to our ears in credit card debt. She was a habitual shopper.

"If she got bored, she would shop. If she was out on the town, she would shop. She always found reasons. We had separate closets, and hers got so full at one point that she started sneaking new clothes, purses, and shoes into mine.

"It didn't stop with just clothes. Had it stopped there, I might have been able to live with it, but she was the type that wanted the best of everything. Everything had to be new and perfect. She wanted the nicest cars, the finest dinners, and so on. Nothing was ever enough.

"Pretty soon, I put my foot down. I cut off her credit cards and took her name off the account. I had no choice. She was going to break me. After that, the sex turned cold, and the 'I love you' faded away. We were just a shell of the couple we were when we dated. The relationship soured. So, I finally filed for divorce.

"It became clear to me that she only married me for one reason. I wasn't going to live my life as someone's bank, and that's all I was to her." Somehow telling Quinn all of this makes me feel even closer to her. Phil already knows why we divorced, as does my family, but for some reason, telling someone out loud takes a load off my shoulders that I've been carrying for two years, and it feels good knowing it was her I told. I'm not sure why I feel so comfortable with her, especially when I know she can turn on a dime, but still, it feels good.

"That's terrible. I feel sorry for her."

"For *her*?"

"Sure. That's a terrible way to go through life. Never loving anyone. Just using them. She must be quite a lonely person."

I had never thought of it that way. I had never considered that Lisa was as miserable in our relationship as I was.

"Don't get me wrong, I definitely feel sorry for you, too," she says, "but you have an advantage that she obviously doesn't."

"What might that be?"

She glances up at me. "The ability to love someone for who she truly is and not just what she can give you. You can look past someone's ego and faults."

"How do you know?"

"Because you look past mine every day."

I hesitate. "It's part of our deal."

"It is, but I don't think you believe that."

"Tell me about your ex," I say, trying to change the subject.

"Spencer. Spencer, like Lisa, was perfect. He just stayed perfect a little longer than Lisa did. I started dating him when I was a senior in high school. We got engaged early and married when I was twenty. Then ten years later, out of the blue, he came home and sat me down and told me he had been having an affair with a younger woman.

"He's thirty-seven and she's twenty-one. So, a *much* younger woman. The sad part is I never even suspected. I was blind-sided. I never would have thought Spencer would be capable of cheating.

"Now I know anyone is capable of it, which is why I'm not ready to put myself out there for anyone else just yet. I wasted my youth on him. I never got to go to parties or go out with the girls. I went to high school, got married right out of college, and started working."

It was all starting to come together. All the rules and snide remarks. The no calling the next day. It didn't make sense to me at the time, but it does now.

————

SHE LEAVES SHORTLY after our discussion, and I'm left

with the same lost feeling I'm always left with after being with her. What did she mean earlier when she said she didn't think I "believed that?" Did she mean that she believes I want more from her? Or did she mean that she wants more from me?

I understand her a bit better now, but she always seems to say or do something that leaves my mind in shambles. Each time I see her, I feel happy and exhilarated, but nearly every time she leaves, it's as if she tries to leave me confused. Is she doing it on purpose? I'm beginning to think it's because when we are together, she feels close to me, but when it's time for her to leave, she panics and wants to make sure I know this is all part of our original agreement.

How can I get her past that? What can I do to make her comfortable enough to see past her fears? I'm not Spencer.

I wouldn't hurt her. Not on purpose. Though now I think of what Janine said. No matter what, someone will probably get hurt.

10

QUINN

"THERE'S no way to pack for this trip," I say, slinging a random shirt into my bag.

"Relax. I'll help you," Fran says, calmly folding a pair of my red shorts. "Besides, I picked you up something for our trip." I peek up to find her holding up a white bathing suit. The problem? There's barely any "suit" to it.

"Fran, I can't wear that! His family is going to be there, for goodness sake."

"C'mon Quinn. I'm trying to live vicariously through you. Besides, I'm sure his family won't be in the hot tub with you," she comments, wiggling her brows.

I snatch the suit from her, shoving it to the bottom on my bag. "I have no sex life yet, remember? If you want a sex life, Phil will be there, and I'm sure he wouldn't mind helping you out," I say with a smile.

"You know, I hate you a little bit more every day."

I laugh. "We'll be on vacation, Fran. I'm pretty sure he won't ask for your hand in marriage if you wanted to get a little frisky after wine one night. We're staying beach front. You could make love right in the water."

"Yeah, right, and pick something up from him that soap can't wash off. No, thank you."

I close my eyes and laugh, shaking my head. "You're so twisted."

———

FRAN HELPS me pack for another hour, and I can't help but check the time every five minutes. We're supposed to meet Brett at his apartment building at noon, and the three of us will catch a taxi to John F. Kennedy airport in New York City. The plane departs two hours after, and then there's no turning back. Six hours later, I'll be in Malibu.

"You ready?" Fran asks, reaching for the doorknob.

I glance around my house, my safe zone. All the lights have been turned out, the beds are made, and Evie is safe with Spencer. I suck in a breath and feel my chest rise. "I'm ready."

"You're sure?"

I nod.

We wheel our bags down the walkway to the taxicab awaiting us. The whole ride to Brett's apartment, I feel like I'm going to be sick, but it isn't until we pull up in front of his apartment that the nervousness sets in.

"Well, we're past the point of no return," Fran says, opening her door. I wonder why she isn't as nervous as me. She has to lie just as much. Does she realize that?

I slow down my breathing by telling myself that if Fran's not nervous, then there's no reason for me to be. We have each other, and if push comes to shove, Brett will have my back too. Maybe even Phil because Phil knows his week there only lasts for as long as we keep the charade going. I call Brett from the cab to tell him we've arrived, and Fran and I sit waiting for him.

"I don't know if I can do this," I mutter.

"You can," she assures me. "You already convinced them."

"I put on a sham for a couple of hours, not a whole week."

"Look," she says, taking my hand. "I'm here with you. We get an all-expense paid vacation to Malibu, and if I can deal with Phil the whole time, you can definitely handle Brett."

"Okay. Okay. You're right."

"Hello ladies," Brett says after opening the door. I scoot to the middle to allow him to slide in, and he puts his hand across me to shake Fran's. "Hello again, Fran. It's good to see you."

"Likewise," she says with her palm down, as if he's going to kiss the top of her hand. I shoot my eyes at her, and she chuckles. She thinks because he's paying for the trip he must be rich, and in her eyes, that means he's basically royalty. I'm surprised she didn't get out of the cab and curtsy.

"You girls ready for this?"

"Sure," I say, though I'm not.

"Definitely," says Fran, and I can't help but eye her just a bit for her optimism.

"And Fran," says Brett. "I'm sorry in advance for anything Phil says, does, or hints to."

"Don't worry. I know how to handle boys like Phil."

I laugh softly at her referring to him as a mere boy, but only because it's true. Brett gets a chuckle from it as well.

The light humor gives me a sense of relief and hopefully a taste of what the trip will be like. I hope it's as lighthearted as this. Only time will tell.

"Oh, I forgot to tell you girls. My family will be on a different flight, so we'll arrive at the beach house a few hours before them. That will give you time to relax, unpack, and freshen up. Whatever you want to do," he says.

"What about Phil?" I ask.

He smirks. "Phil will unfortunately be on our flight. Fran, I'm sorry to say you'll have to sit with him. Quinn and I need to make sure we have time to get to know as much as we can about one another before we deal with my family for the week."

Fran lets out a sigh. I don't blame her.

"Hopefully," he says, "they're already past the asking a million questions phase, but that remains to be seen. Better safe than sorry, but to make up for it, Fran, we are flying first class, as requested."

"Oh, Brett, you didn't have to fly us first class. Fran was just teasing about that."

"No, I wasn't," she spits out

I cringe and glance to Brett, but he just chuckles and waves his hand in a manner to let me know it's okay.

———

IN NO TIME AT ALL, we've boarded the plane, and Phil is already ordering champagne for himself and Fran. To my surprise, Fran is smiling and laughing with him. I hide my amusement at their exchange.

"Would you like some champagne as well?" Brett asks.

I shrug. "I've never had champagne before."

"Then you have to have try it."

Moments later, he's handing me my own tall glass of bubbly, golden champagne. "To making memories," he says holding up his glass.

Our glasses clink together, and I giggle into my drink as the bubbles tickle my nose. Fran smiles at me from across the aisle and holds her glass up to toast me. I hold mine up as well.

The whole flight is a mixture of flowing champagne and learning tidbits about one another. Brett's lived in Manhattan his whole life, and that's the true reason his bar is such a success. He knows so many people, as does his family. I, on the other hand, divulge that I moved to New York City because Spencer was offered a job there shortly after we married. Originally, I'm from Louisiana.

I tell him I moved to Manhattan after Spencer and I separated, although I don't tell him it was mostly for Evie's sake. I still haven't told him I have a daughter, and I don't intend to.

He tells me what it was like growing up with a twin sister, and I tell him all about how my brother's band, The Blue Man Blues, got started. We talk about my failed attempt to fix Fran up with my brother, which leads to him telling me about his brother-in-law, Russ.

"So, would you say Phil is your best friend?" I ask him.

"Yeah, I suppose so. He's my oldest friend. Believe it or not, if you can look past the cheap tricks and flashy clothes, he's a good guy."

I glance over to see Fran laughing. I can't tell if she's honestly amused by what Phil is saying or if the champagne has her judgment clouded. There's something honest about the smile I see on Phil's face as he delves further into whatever tall tale he's selling her.

"I can believe that. Everyone has their own persona, I suppose. Maybe he's just afraid of getting hurt if he shows who he truly is."

"I think he's afraid of rejection. He can't stand it when he thinks someone doesn't like him or if he thinks someone is upset with him. I think that's why he tries so hard with Fran."

Makes sense. He's a male version of me. He's afraid to get hurt, so he plays as if he's someone he truly isn't. I feel oddly connected to Phil after hearing this and a little relieved that Fran seems to be giving him what he needs to feel accepted.

———

WHEN WE LAND AT LAX, we rent a car to drive to the beach house an hour away. Fran and I take the back seat.

"You seem to be getting pretty cozy with Phil," I point out.

"Honey, I'm so pumped full of champagne right now I'd be cozy with Santa Claus."

I laugh. "Real nice, Fran. I think Phil is a good guy underneath it all. At least that's what Brett says."

She shrugs. "Well, I'm not going to offer to be his booty buddy like you, but I'll try to be on my best behavior."

I chuckle. "Good."

We arrive at the beach house, and I'm in awe. It's a two-story white house with long glass windows and a teal front door. It sits right on the beach, just as Brett described. We step out of the car to the sound of crashing waves and the sweet smell of salty water. The sun is beating down on my skin, and I can almost feel my body soaking up the vitamin D. The breeze blows my hair, and I peek back to Brett who is getting out of the other car.

Fran is smiling from ear to ear, and I hear an enthusiastic "Yeah, buddy!" coming from Phil.

"Do I deliver, or do I deliver?" Brett asks, suddenly at my side.

I wipe stray hairs from my face and smile—my first real one in days. "You deliver."

He chuckles. "Come on. Let's go in."

Walking into the house makes me question if Brett *is* royalty. The walls are painted a faint blue, and a vase filled to the brim with sea shells sits on almost every table. Cream leather furniture fills the living room, and an antique dining table sits off the immaculate kitchen, which seems to go on for miles.

"Is this where you always stay when you come?" I ask Brett.

He laughs. "Well, yeah. It's my parent's house."

"You mean you didn't rent this?" asks Fran.

"No way," says Phil, clapping Brett's shoulder. "My man's got the hook-up."

"Come on," he tells me. "I'll show you girls where we'll all be sleeping."

I already know I'll be bunking with Brett for appearances' sake, but I start to question whether Fran and Phil are supposed to be a couple as well. That would probably send her over the edge, and as someone who has seen her over the edge before, I'm not looking forward to it. He takes us up a wooden staircase, and bedroom doors line a wide hallway full of pictures.

I can see previous years' vacation pictures and childhood pictures of Brett and Anne. They were so cute. I can't imagine what a handful having twins was for his mother.

"Phil, yours is down the hall to the right. Fran you're directly across from him. Ours is this way," he tells me, taking me by the hand. I give a little nod to Fran as we part ways. She offers me a wink that lifts my spirits just a bit.

My spirit returns when we walk into the room. I gasp uncontrollably as Brett flings his duffel bag onto the bed, which is metal with a sheer white canopy. Metal roses are engraved around the headboard, which make it seem even more romantic. The dresser is made of mirrored glass and decorated with light blue candles and antique perfume bottles. There's a flat-screen TV hanging in the corner of the room and a full-length mirror, which matches the dresser's glass design.

"Let me get that for you," he offers, taking my bag from my willing hand.

"You stay here once a year?" I ask in amazement. "How can you ever tear yourself away from this place?"

He chuckles. "After spending a week with my family, you'll see just how easy it can be."

I raise my eyebrows. I hadn't thought of that. Honestly, I

had forgotten for a few wonderful moments that it wasn't just going to be the four of us here. Now *that* would have been nice.

I start unpacking and catch a glance of Brett. He's smiling. He has such a great smile. I begin putting my clothes carefully in the dresser, as if I'm afraid it will break, when Fran enters our room through the opened door.

"Quinn, have you ever seen anything—hey, your room is even nicer than mine!" she exclaims, running her fingers over the top of the dresser.

"Who cares?" says Phil entering after her. "It's not like we'll be spending a lot of time in our rooms."

"True," she admits.

Brett has now begun helping me unpack, but I hadn't noticed until he holds up the skimpy, inappropriate bathing suit Fran bought me. I snatch it from his hands in embarrassment.

"Don't mind that. It is just one of Fran's sick jokes," I say eying her. She smirks but hides it with her hand. "I don't plan on wearing it. I have another bathing suit in there."

"Don't worry," he says. "I know a place where you can wear it where no one else will see ... besides me," he assures me with a flash of his teeth.

A small laugh escapes me. Suddenly my cell phone rings, and I dig it from my purse to see that it's Thomas. In all the nervousness and excitement, I had forgotten to call him before I left like he asked me to, but now that I'm with everyone, I can't answer the phone.

It just doesn't seem right. I hastily mute my phone and shove it back in my purse.

"Who was that?" asks Fran.

"Thomas."

"Why didn't you answer it?"

"I'll call him back later."

As Fran and Phil file out of the room, Brett takes me by the elbow pulling me back. "You don't have to dodge your friends when you're with me."

"I'm not."

He searches my face for a moment. "Okay."

First chance I get, I need to talk to Fran alone. She knows Thomas and me better than anyone. I need her advice about Thomas and Brett both—desperately.

11

BRETT

"DID you see the way Fran was flirting with me on the plane?" Phil whispers as we make our way back downstairs.

"I saw you filling her glass full of alcohol the entire trip," I say with a knowing eye.

"Hey, she asked for the champagne. I was just there to toast with her."

"Any more and you would have become her babysitter."

"Mmm, I do love a woman who can drink," he says, staring up at the ceiling as if praying to the liquor gods.

"Probably because that's the only kind you've ever been with—drunk and loose."

"You bite your tongue," he demands. "I've been with many a woman who weren't... loose."

I laugh, and he joins in. More times than not, the women Phil entices are tipsy, if not drunk. It's not that they have to be to find Phil attractive or even want to sleep with him, it's just that Phil *thinks* they have to be drunk to want him. If he didn't have the persona of a sleaze ball, he'd attract more women, but I can't tell him that.

"How long do we have before your folks get here?" Quinn asks.

I glance at my watch, and a sinking feeling takes hold of my stomach. "Any minute now, I imagine." She squints at me, and I know she must recognize the concern in my voice, but I just clap my hands together nervously. "Don't worry, guys. Usually we spend the first day just lying on the beach.

"Sounds heavenly," Fran says with raised eyebrows, the dimples in her cheeks giving away her stifled grin.

"It does sound nice," Quinn says, still taking in her surroundings, enamored by the beauty of it all. A big piece of me is glad I was able to give her this today.

Our bums barely touch the leather seats of the living room sofa before we hear a cheerful "Hello, dears!" from the front door. My mother and father file in with their suitcases, along with Anne, Russ, and Nell.

"Uncle Brett!" yells Nell, and I scoop her up in a hug. My mother, on the other hand, heads straight for Quinn.

"Hello, darling! I'm so glad you could make it. We've all been looking forward to getting to know you better," she exclaims, hugging Quinn.

"How are you, Mrs. Redding? It's wonderful to see you again."

"Oh, please, call me Kathryn!" she says with a final rub of Quinn's back. My mother is such a lovely woman. She's on the short side, at just over five feet, and her hair is all but silver now from the years of dealing with twins, but if I can find a woman who is half as sweet and caring as she is, I'll feel like I've done something right with my life.

"Okay, Kathryn. This is my friend, Fran," says Quinn.

"Oh, another beautiful lady!" she says, skipping a formal handshake and going straight in for a hug.

"So nice to meet you, Kathryn. You have a lovely home."

"Why thank you, Fran! You two are the kindest young ladies," she boasts, pinching their cheeks lightly. Both girls smile largely. It didn't take my mom long to fall in love. The knot in my stomach has relaxed, and I watch as everyone meets Fran and tells Quinn how glad they are that she came.

Russ, Dad, and I stay in the shadows, although the guys offered a quick hello to them as well. My father is a stocky man who still has a head full of black hair, which is where Anne and I get ours. Russ is the complete opposite: on the skinny side with blond hair and tanned skin. Phil is eating it all up today, winking at me, and I see him put his arm around Fran's shoulders, but she brushes it off quickly as she meets everyone.

I stifle a grin. She'll come around. It takes a strong woman to resist Phil for too long. Especially when there's wine in the house.

"Why don't you guys head upstairs and put on your swimwear while we unpack? We'll meet you out there straight away."

"Sounds good, Mom," I say, kissing her forehead. I reach out for Quinn's hand, and I see her chest rise as if she's breathing heavily at the idea of holding my hand. I give her a knowing look, and she accepts it as we make our way upstairs, Phil and Fran trailing behind us.

"So, you going to wear this?" I say, playfully holding up what might have been sold as a swimsuit but looks more like sex shop paraphernalia.

"No," she cringes, yanking it from my hands. "I can imagine what your mother would think of me then." She sticks it in the bottom dresser drawer beneath a few other articles of clothing. "I'm going to wear *this* one," she boasts, holding up a blue, tasteful two-piece.

I shrug. "I guess that'll do."

She jerks her head back. "What does that mean?"

"Nothing!" My eyes cut back to her.

Quinn wraps a towel around herself after changing, as though she is modest, and we head out the door, meeting Fran and Phil in the hall. I can't help but close my eyes as tightly as they will go at the sight of Phil.

"Phil, what's the deal man?"

"What?" he says.

"He wonders why I can't take him seriously," Fran snaps.

"Oh, Phil," Quinn says.

I kid you not, he is in the skimpiest swim suit a man has ever worn, and if my eyes have not deceived me, I am not the only one who has had a "porn star wax" as Phil called it days ago. It's not that Phil doesn't have a nice body—he does. I admit that in a totally heterosexual way. Regardless, my mother is going to be accompanying us later, and Phil is wearing something that barely covers his junk. With it, only a gold chain around his neck glittering in a thick, black mound of chest hair, which matches the hair on his head and the two-day stubble on his chin.

"I don't want a tan line around my thighs. Sue me!" he says loudly, trudging down the stairs without so much as a towel around his waist. Fran shakes her head, and Quinn can't help but giggle into my arm as she stands beside me.

"Well, no one said this trip was going to be easy," I tell them, which only makes Quinn giggle harder. I finally crack and laugh with her, and Fran joins in, stealing Quinn away from my arm and hightailing it down the stairs. I shake my head and follow.

———

WE SETTLE UNDER AN UMBRELLA, lying in beach chairs, and Quinn asks me to rub sunscreen on her fair skin. I jump at the chance. I smooth the creamy substance over her shoulders and massage it in. I take note that this is seeming a bit more erotic to me than it should. I run my hands down her back and over her sides.

I glance down at the small of her back. What is it about the small of a woman's back that drives me crazy? I'm not sure, but heaven help me as I pass over that spot and glance up at her fair neck as she holds her hair up. I lean in and steal a kiss on her neck slowly.

She doesn't jerk away or tell me no. My arms find their way around her, rubbing the rest of the lotion from my hands onto her stomach. She sighs deeply. She peeks behind her to meet my eyes.

"There's a changing tent over there," she says.

This jolts me back to reality. "Nope. You know the rules."

She sighs, letting her hair fall.

Still, I lean in to give her a last kiss, but she stops me, and I know already what that means. Kissing is now off-limits. I throw the bottle of lotion down on the ground and lean back in my chair.

"What's wrong with you?" she asks.

I face her. "Like always, you have to do something to ruin the moment."

"Here I thought *you* were trying to ruin it," she snaps.

"*Me?* You can't be serious. How was I trying to ruin it?"

"By breaking the rules."

"Well, I'm so sorry," I spit out sarcastically. "I wasn't aware that kissing you was against the rules, but now I know, and it won't happen again." I stand to walk away, and she catches my arm.

"Okay. Okay, I'm sorry. I never said it was against the rules, I know. I just want to make sure we don't pass that line drawn in the sand."

"What line would that be?"

"The line between lovers and a couple."

I shake my head, eying her. "That would never happen. You'd never allow it."

She recoils back an inch as if my words hurt her. She lowers her head. "I don't want to fight, Brett. I can't tell you how hard this week will be without you on my side."

I take a deep breath. Finally, I see a bit of vulnerability. Finally, she admits she needs *something* from me. "I *am* on your side. I'm *always* on your side, Quinn."

She looks me in the eye for only a moment and pulls me back down, putting her arms around me and embracing me in a gentle hug. She kisses my cheek. "Thank you."

I glance to Phil who has lowered his sunglasses on the bridge of his nose and winks at Fran.

"There's a changing tent over there," he tells her with a wink.

"Not even in your wildest dream," Fran spits out, never bothering to make eye contact.

I hear him trying to coax her with promises of multiple orgasms. Quinn giggles once more, and I laugh at her delight in their exchange.

It's only after we rested that Fran talks us all into a dip in the water. We swim and lie on our backs, allowing our bodies to float in the warm, salty water. We act like teenagers, allowing the girls to sit on our shoulders as they fight to push each other off. I can't remember ever having this much fun with Lisa. Come to think of it, after we got married, it seemed the fun stopped. Maybe that's what Quinn is so afraid of. In the restaurant, she spoke of walking down the aisle and playing the "game" before, and I remember her saying, "Now I just want to have fun."

It makes me wonder if married people are incapable of being fun. I see my parents laughing with one another, so I know it's possible, but since Quinn's father left when she was young, and her mother is now gone, I bet she never got the chance to see them having fun together, if they ever did. All she knows of marriage is her experience with Spencer.

Other than my parents, all I know of marriage is the sad excuse of one I shared with Lisa. She refused to even make love to me on our wedding night, saying she was too tired from the day's affairs. I was tired that day, too, but I couldn't see not consummating our marriage on our wedding night. It didn't seem to bother her.

Come to think of it, once we did finally make love, it was robotic and cold. Without a promise of some sort of future together, I wonder how long Quinn will keep me around before she tires of me.

12

QUINN

"SO, Quinn, Brett tells us you're originally from Louisiana," Kathryn says, cutting her steak into tiny pieces.

"Yes, ma'am. Born and raised. I moved to New York City with my ex-husband, but moved to Manhattan after our divorce."

"It's so sad when marriages don't work out. Especially for young people. It's so good to see you aren't the kind to let it define you," she admits, taking a small bite and chewing delicately and more ladylike than I ever have. Her words hit close to home. I suppose I have let it define me, but is that so wrong?

Aren't we supposed to learn from our mistakes and rectify them? I'm almost offended by her statement, though I don't show it. I cut my food in tiny pieces as well, but only so I can appear as ladylike as she thinks I am. I'm so hungry tonight that picking the steak up with my hands and burying my face in it sounds more satisfying.

"So, Anne, Brett tells me you're twins. Which of you is the eldest?" I say with an awkward smile, hoping to avoid any more questions about me.

"Oh, that's a state secret apparently," she laughs.

"I don't understand." I laugh nervously.

"Mother refuses to tell us, despite our years of hounding her," Brett chimes in before taking a huge bite of steak, which leaves me quite jealous.

I chuckle. "Why is that?"

"Just to tick them off." Kathryn chuckles, as do I.

"So, Joe," I ask his father, "you never whispered it to them behind your wife's back?"

He laughs a bit. "I wouldn't dream of betraying my wife's trust, even for the smallest of information. Besides, it's much more fun, them not knowing."

That's the most I've heard the man speak since I arrived, and I'm feeling mildly triumphant that I'm the one who got him to talk. Brett wasn't kidding about his dad being a man of few words.

To my delight, we finish dinner without any more talk of my ex. I would rather not think of him at the moment. I do enough of that on my own. Still, I haven't been able to get Fran alone to discuss Spencer and Thomas. What were the odds that both men would admit their love for me on the same day? Thomas for the first time, and Spencer for the first time since meeting Melissa.

Night comes, and I tell Brett that I want to have some girl time alone with Fran. So, Fran and I change back into our swimsuits and go out to the beach for a late-night swim. The night has cooled off, and light from the moon dances off the water as we soak.

"I'm so glad we get some alone time. Seriously, spending all this time with Phil today had me contemplating homicide. Prison can't be that bad, right?"

I chuckle. Fran is much more petite than I am, with darker skin. Honestly, seeing her in her skimpy swimsuit today made me a bit self-conscious of my own body.

"So, I have to talk to you about something," I tell her.

"Well, go on then," she says, leaning back in the water to wet her hair.

"I think Spencer wants me back." Her head pops up quickly, and her eyes are round. The light from the moon makes her blue eyes seem piercing, and I can almost feel them burning a hole through my own.

She tilts her head. "Why would you think that?"

I give a nonchalant motion with my head and stretch out my arms over the water, allowing my fingers to float on top. "He more or less told me."

"Quinn, no."

"No, what?"

"Quinn, I know you, and I know what you're thinking, and trust me when I say, going back to Spencer would *not* be what's best for Evie."

I wipe down my face with my wet hand but only so I can hide my face for the briefest of moments—afraid that she can see right through me.

"He's a wonderful father," I remind her.

"He can stay a wonderful father. That doesn't mean he makes a wonderful husband. Quinn, if he cheats once, he is sure to do it again."

"I'm not sure I believe that."

"Quinn, he's been shacked up with Melissa for months now."

"Maybe that's because I didn't fight hard enough for him."

"He was your husband! You're not supposed to have to fight for your own husband. Really, you're not supposed to have to fight for a boyfriend. When you make a commitment to some-one, that's supposed to be it!"

I scratch the back of my neck as if her words are making my skin crawl. Part of me feels like she's right, but there's another part that makes me think Spencer got all the cheating out of his system and is sorry. "There's more," I tell her.

"Oh, no. I'm not sure I can take more, Quinn."

I roll my eyes. "It's Thomas."

She perks up. "What about him."

"He admitted that *he* loves me."

Her eyes widen once more, and she leans in. "Thomas?"

I nod.

She shakes her head slowly in disbelief. "Why now? Why is he just now saying something?"

I shrug. "I don't know why. Maybe he's just confused or doesn't want to see me get hurt. He told me he didn't want to see me sell myself short by using some random guy just for sex."

Now she's the one wiping her face to hide her expression.

"What a mess," she moans.

"Yeah," I say, scratching my neck again. Maybe I should just peel my skin off.

"What are you going to do about that?"

"What *can* I do? I don't feel anything romantic for Thomas."

"But you do for Spencer?"

I shrug. "I don't know about right now, but I'm sure I could in time."

"You want to know what I think?" she asks. I nod. "I think you should actually give Brett a chance."

"Oh, come on, Fran."

"I mean it! Look how perfect he is! He's mature and owns his own business. You'd get to take trips and see the world. I mean, Randy is already playing at his bar. You don't think that's a little bit of fate nipping you on the butt?"

My lips purse together in reflex to her words. "Brett and I can never be in a relationship."

"Tell me why, Quinn. Don't you see the way he looks at you?"

"He knows I'm broken."

"Yes, and *still* he looks at you."

I shake my head. "Even if I decided I wanted a relationship with him, I couldn't. Not now. Not after all of *this*," I say flailing my arms in the air.

She stares at me with a stone-like expression. "I wish I knew what went on in your mind. Promise me when you die you'll donate your brain to science, because only a scientist could understand what goes on up there."

I roll my eyes.

"I'm going back inside," she says, walking through the now chilly water up to the beach. I follow, though I wish I had nerve enough to drown myself at this point. Ugh!

WHEN I ARRIVE BACK to the room, the skimpy white bathing suit that Fran bought me is sprawled out neatly on the bed. Standing in the door of our connected bathroom is Brett in all his perfectness wearing only a towel and a smile. Steam escapes from the room where he just showered "I laid out your suit."

"I see that," I say. "What for?"

"It's hot tub time."

It does feel nice to be wanted in some way. Spencer never wanted me so much. I always assumed something was wrong with me. Maybe I wasn't sexy or adventurous enough. Maybe that's why I feel so justified in the way I conduct my and Brett's relationship.

I'm leaving a bit of mystery. Something to be desired. Of course, if I'm right, he desires more from me than I do him.

He may have agreed to the terms, but if Fran is right, he's looking for more from me than just a fake fiancé followed by sex.

The hot tub is outside, just out the sliding glass door, where Brett assures me no one comes. I sink effortlessly into the water and wish I had a hot towel over my face to complete the feeling. I lean my head back and close my eyes.

"You did good today," he says.

I don't open my eyes. "I tried."

"You succeeded." There's a pause. "Look, I'm sorry about this afternoon. I don't want you to give me anything you don't feel comfortable with. Not even a kiss."

I open my eyes and glance up at the stars. You don't see stars like this in Manhattan. Why does everything out of his mouth have to be so perfect? It's just like that day in the hotel room. He knows me too well and seems to sense what I need to do and what I need to hear.

"It's okay. I shouldn't have pushed you away. It's normal, I suppose, to want to kiss someone after spending so much time together. I just can't get that close to someone. Not yet. What did you ask me out here for?"

He peers down, his arms stretched out to the sides, resting them on the back of the hot tub. "I don't know. I just feel like you need a friend tonight."

"I already have a friend here."

"Well, I thought you could use one more. We *can* be friends, Quinn. I won't push you to do anything you don't want to do."

I find myself scooting closer to him, right underneath his arm. I lay my head on him. "Thank you," is all I can muster.

"Can I put my arm around you?" he asks. Can he? Will I be okay with that? Will it make me uncomfortable? I came this far.

"Yeah, you can do that." His warm arm rests gently around

me, and our feet intertwine in the water. I need this tonight. Just to be held with no expectations.

It's just one friend holding another because she needs it. He said he wouldn't force me into anything. He won't rush me into anything I'm not ready for. He understands, and still he's here and wants to be around me. Maybe I am broken.

I think Fran is right, and Brett cares for me. I don't see how. I'm such a mess. All I do is push him away. I wouldn't put up with that from someone, but here he is doing it.

Fran seems to think it has nothing to do with his just holding up his side of the bargain. Maybe it doesn't, but after this trip is over, what do I do with that information? I don't want to hurt someone the way I've been hurt, nor force myself into a relationship.

When this trip is over, I'll have to part ways with Brett. I can't hurt someone so sweet or carry on like this when I know I can't give him more than I already am, even if he does agree to it. Right now, though, in this moment, it feels good just to be held by someone who might care about me.

13

BRETT

AFTER A LONG DAY, I decide to do something special for Quinn—to the annoyance of Phil. He's been suspicious of her from day one, though he is just now giving me an earful about it.

"How do you know though, Brett?"

"I just do."

"I'm tellin' you, man. The chick is only in this for your money. Just like Lisa."

"Quinn is nothing like Lisa."

"What do you know about her?"

"I know enough."

"She asks you for sex, and you start buying her diamond rings and getaways, and you stand there and tell me you know for a fact she isn't just keeping you so you will give her more."

"Phil, she didn't want any of this. She wanted a plain band for a wedding ring. I gave her the diamond one because you and I both know my parents know me better. I would have never proposed with a band. C'mon. Plus, it reminded her of her mother, whom she lost not long ago, if you care to know."

"Well, she sure agreed to the getaway fast. Wait... it reminded her of her mother?"

I grimace. I already know where this is going. I can't seem to keep my big foot out of my mouth. That's my problem. It's becoming a habit.

"You're falling for this chick."

"I'm not. I'm simply a good person. If I weren't, I would have fired you from the bar long ago."

"On what grounds?" he laughs.

"Come on, Phil. You drink more of the liquor than you serve."

He tilts his head to the ceiling as if he is above justifying my allegation. "I don't know what you are talking about, sir."

I laugh. "I'm sure you don't."

"You know what your problem is, don't you?" he says.

"Enlighten me."

"Your heart is bigger than your brain."

"And that's a problem?"

"Yes, and apparently frequently. Most of all with women. That's why Lisa ruled your life for two years." As he lectures me on the difference between using my brain and using my heart, I'm steadily running a nice hot bath for Quinn, though she doesn't know it. I know how women love baths, and this new claw-foot tub my mother put in is just perfect.

I pick up a box of matches lying on the counter and light a few candles, placing them on the floor at the corners of the tub and dimming the overhead lights. I hear Anne and Quinn coming up the stairs. Anne invited Quinn out earlier for a swim to get to know her better, and I marveled at the idea—although truthfully, I was a little worried if Quinn would be able to keep up the charade with my sister. When I hear them giggling as they come up the stairs though, my worries are put to rest.

"Nice time, ladies?" I ask.

"Very nice time," Quinn says, walking into the bedroom past me.

Anne merely whispers, "I like this one, Brett," before turning to go to her own room. I motion for her to go.

"Oh, were you about to take a bath?" Quinn asks, having stepped into the bathroom.

"No, no. I ran that bath for you. I figured you'd want to wash off the sea water before dinner."

The smile my sister put on her face has now dwindled slowly away, and I hear her swallow hard. I see tears filling her eyes, and I almost pat myself on the back for being romantic enough to bring a woman to tears.

"I can run my own baths, Brett."

My brows pull together in confusion. "I know that, I was just... just trying to do something nice for you. Something a friend would do."

"Friends don't run one another candlelit baths. This is too much. I can't be this person for you. Don't you understand?" Her voice a yelling whisper.

I shake my head slowly in disbelief or confusion, I'm not sure which—maybe both. "Why are you getting angry? I was just trying to do something nice for you."

"I don't need you to," she says, stomping off.

"Where are you going?"

"Downstairs to take a shower in the guest bath." Just like that, she's gone.

Phil pokes his head out of his bedroom, having heard the whole messy affair. He stares at me, still standing in the doorway in shock.

"I stand corrected," he jokes. "No woman who's trying to keep you would act like that. Obviously, you don't know her as well as you think you do."

I walk inside the bedroom and toss a towel on the bed, sitting on the edge myself. "Guess not. I can't win with this girl."

He sits on the bed beside me and claps my shoulder. "The

question you need to ask yourself is why are you even trying to?"

I do need to ask myself that question, but all I can think about is how a person can get so mad from a single gesture of friendship.

I promised her I wouldn't do anything she wasn't ready for, but drawing her a bath? *That* sent her over the edge? Until now, she seemed to be taking everything in stride, but apparently the bath was the straw that broke the camel's back.

I think that maybe she is being honest when she says she just wants to use me for sex, but last night in the hot tub, I could have sworn there was more to it than that. Does this girl even know what she wants? I take a step forward, she pushes me two steps back, and tonight it is two *big* steps back.

"What happened?" asks Fran, now standing in the doorway.

"Apparently, your friend is more of a shower person," Phil says, standing and walking from the room.

Fran stands over me, as my head finds my hands. "What happened?"

I chuckle sarcastically. "No idea. I ran her a bath, and she freaked out. You know Quinn better than anyone," I say, removing my hands from my head as she sits down beside me. "What am I doing wrong here? What does she want from me?"

"I don't know what Quinn wants. Honestly, she's thrown me for a loop lately, too. This is a whole new side to her that I've never seen before."

"Well, that helps," I huff to myself.

"I can tell you what she needs though."

I feel my heart jump slightly at her words. "What?"

"Patience. She's going through something right now that we can't understand. She's going through something that *she* can't even understand. We have to be patient with her. *You* have to be patient with her.

"I'm sure you've caught glimpses of what she's truly like, and this whole sex in exchange for being your fiancé... it just came at a bad time in her life."

"Okay. I'll have patience then."

"Can I ask you something?"

I shrug. "Yeah."

"What do *you* want?"

No one has asked me that question before. I want so much— so much I can't say.

"I just want to be close to her."

"Then stop giving her reasons to push you away."

I swallow hard. I didn't know that's what I was doing. I've thought before that I take one step forward and she pushes me two steps back, but it never crossed my mind that I shouldn't take that step forward to begin with. I told her I wouldn't push her, but that's what I've been doing.

At first I was pushing her to move closer into a relationship, and now I'm pushing her to at least have a friendship. Maybe she just wants me to stand still until she figures out what she wants from me, if not just sex.

"Okay," I tell her.

———

WE MEET DOWNSTAIRS FOR DINNER, and Quinn is back to her chipper self, though I'm not. I'm faking it, as I'm sure she is.

"Brett, you've got a keeper right there," says Anne, before sipping her wine. "She had me laughing the whole time we visited today."

"I think so, too," Mom agrees. "You are just the loveliest of girls, Quinn," she acknowledges, patting her hand.

"Thank you. It's easy to be myself around you all. Thank

you so much for having Fran and me here. It's beautiful." Is she actually being herself right now? Or is she just selling herself like she has since they all walked through the door?

I flash back to the look on her face as she got out of the car that first day. I think that's what Fran was speaking of. I got a peek of what she's truly like when her face lit up and she marveled at the beautiful scenery and house.

Then the day Phil wore his skimpy swim suit, she giggled into my arm to keep from laughing out loud at him. It was a good feeling to see her happy. I have caught glimpses of her being herself. And I can tell the difference. Right now, she's just playing her role.

"Let's make a toast," Anne says, holding up her glass. The rest of the family follows suit. "To new friends and soon-to-be new family."

"Here, here," says Mom.

"Cheers!" holler the rest. I join in, but only for appearances' sake. It's then that I feel a foot under the table, and I peek under the table ever so slyly to see that it's Quinn's foot. I glance to her, and her face has an expression on it I've never seen before. It seems apologetic.

I give her a nod and rub my foot against hers as if to let her know that nothing is lost and everything is okay. I still don't understand, but I can't fault her for something simply because I don't understand it. Fran says Quinn's going through something, and I want to be her friend. So, all I can do at this point is let her come to me.

So, she did, with the touch of a foot. A small gesture, but a gesture nonetheless. Maybe Phil was right, and my heart is bigger than my brain, but I don't think that's a bad thing, and I don't think my brain and heart are playing against one another.

I think Phil assumes my brain is saying to ditch the chick while my heart is reaching out to her, but they are working together. My brain is telling me she is going through something that no one but her can understand, and my heart is simply agreeing and lying in wait for her to make her move, for her to be ready. No, my heart and brain aren't at war in the least. They are in cahoots.

———

TONIGHT IN BED, we both stare up at the ceiling. The window is open, and I hear the water crashing upon the shore and I taste the salt in the air. It's relaxing, but sleep escapes me.

"I'm sorry about today," she admits, breaking the silence.

"I know."

She reaches to where my hands are behind my head and takes one of them in hers. Our fingers intertwine, and she gives my hand a light squeeze. I allow her this. Honestly, I'd allow her anything. For some reason, I melt in her presence.

I don't understand it myself, so I can't expect anyone else to. I know Phil doesn't, though Fran seems to, but there's just something about her being that cries out to me and makes me want to take care of her. Maybe because I know all too well what it's like being broken. Apparently, not as broken as she is.

"I know you were only trying to be nice, but it scared me."

"I understand."

She turns on her side to face me. "I know that's not true. You can't possibly understand me because I can't even understand me right now. It's just that when I saw the bath and the candles and the lights down low and the amount of effort you put into every little detail..."

"I know," I interrupt, "you thought I was being romantic, and that's against the rules."

"It is against the rules, but the problem is I wanted the bath."

I turn my face toward her, and my brows push together. "You did?"

"Yes. No one's ever done something like that for me, something so simple that most people would take it for granted. I pictured myself in the bath, relaxing, a glass of wine in hand, and it scared me. Where you're trying to take me, I can't follow."

I turn on my side to face her. "What *can* you do?"

She closes her eyes for a moment. "Only what I'm doing right now. Every breath I take hurts. Every turn I make is wrong. I can't ask someone to be with me through it. I need to take care of some things by myself. Do you understand?"

I squeeze her hand. "Yeah, I understand. I was just trying to make you breathe easier. Trying to show you friendship."

"I know, but at the moment, there's only so much room in my head and in my heart."

I nod slightly, though I'm not sure if she can see it, the moon's rays being the only light in the room.

"I want you in my life. I'm just not sure how yet, and I'm sorry, but that's the best I can give you right now."

"Okay. Just know that when you're ready, I'm here."

Her eyes twinkle in the moonlight as she stares at me. "Goodnight," she whispers before turning on her other side.

"Goodnight."

14

QUINN

THIS MORNING, while the others lie out on the beach, I tell Brett I'm fighting a headache and need to rest, but not to worry. It wasn't altogether a lie, but maybe a white one. I just need to get my head straight. I feel like my brain is just a pile of goop.

I glance out the living room window to see Fran soaking in the water with Anne and Russ. Phil and Brett are lying on beach chairs with Kathryn and Joe, and Nell is building a sand castle. I close my eyes and consider Fran's opinion from the other night. She thinks I should give Brett more of a chance. I'll say one thing for him: he's understanding. Either that, or he just truly needs a fiancé at the moment.

I open my eyes and observe the family once more. Anne is smiling, and Fran has her head thrown back in laughter. Phil is eying Fran and stands to join in on the watery fun. Brett has picked up a book to read.

I turn my back to the door then walk back to the room and crash onto the bed. Maybe I do have a headache after all, but my phone rings. I check it and see that it's Thomas... again. I never called him back.

"Hello?"

"Hey, what happened to calling me before you left?" he asks.

"I'm sorry. I was in a rush and forgot." Truth.

"Well, I called you the other day. Didn't you get my voicemail?"

"Oh, no. I didn't. I'm sorry." Lie.

"Okay, well at least now I know you made it safely. How's it going?" How's it going? I have no clue. Good? Bad? I'm not sure.

"It's going about as well as can be expected," I admit, peering around at the nicest bedroom I've ever stayed in. "The house is beautiful. Swimming in the ocean is great. Fran seems to be enjoying herself." I chuckle.

"Quinn, have you thought about our talk?"

I sigh. Only every night since it took place. "I haven't been able to give anything much thought, Thomas." Lie. "I'm just trying to get through this trip without ruining this guy's whole world." Truth.

"I could take care of you, Quinn. I would never hurt you like Spencer. I would never use you like Brett."

"Brett isn't using me," I shoot off almost angrily. Why?

There's a heavy pause on the phone, and I kick myself for sounding so forceful. "Then what would you call what he's doing?" he asks.

"Thomas, you forget that I'm the one who initiated the whole situation with Brett."

"No, I haven't forgotten, but a gentleman would have never accepted such an offer."

I roll my eyes instinctively. "Oh, please, Thomas. Don't you dare—"

"You're falling for him," he interrupts.

"What?"

"You're falling in love with Brett."

"Don't be ridiculous." That *is* ridiculous, right? If I were in love, I would know it.

"Then do you love me?" he asks, and I shudder at the question, not because Thomas is the one asking it, but because anyone is asking it. I'm not sure if I'm capable of being in love with anyone at the moment.

"Thomas, I do love you but—"

"No. No buts," he interrupts once more. "You either love me or you don't. If you love me, I will be with you forever. I can promise you that."

"No one can promise that, Thomas."

"Yes, they can. It's called getting married. Marriage is a promise to be with that person forever." Please tell me he's not proposing. I'm not mentally sound enough to deal with something as crazy as that right now.

"Yeah, and look how well that turned out for me the first time." Suddenly Fran appears in the doorway, and I feel my stomach jump. The same feeling you get when you glance in your rearview mirror and find red and blue flashing lights. "I have to go, Thomas, but I'll call you once I'm back home, and we'll talk." I hang up before he can argue.

"Believe it or not, I wasn't eavesdropping," she says.

"No?"

"Nope. So now you have to tell me what Thomas said."

I shake my head in disbelief over the entire phone call. "Oh, you know, same old, same old. A man professing his eternal love for me and promising me the moon. Just another day in the neighborhood."

She shakes her head. "So, Thomas truly is in love with you."

I shrug in annoyance. "I don't know. He seems to think he is, but he also thinks I'm in love with Brett."

"What would make him think that?"

"I defended him, so obviously that means I'm in love with him, I guess."

"Defended him?"

"Thomas accused him of using me."

"You don't think he is?"

"Well, I did until our little talk in the water the other night. I thought everything was going according to plan, but you *want* me to be in love with Brett, and Thomas *thinks* I'm in love with Brett." My head sinks into my hands, and I feel the sudden urge to beat my head against the wall.

"Well, what do *you* think? What do *you* feel?"

My head rises, and I sniff in a heavy gust of air. "I feel like I would be able to figure out how I feel and what I want if everyone would back off and give me time, but everyone is too busy running me baths, telling me who I should love, making me life promises, and announcing their love for me.

"I'm just a ball of emotion and fear. It's getting hard to even function throughout the day, and I still have to make it through the rest of this trip." I close my eyes in frustration and lower my head. "I'll be glad when it's time to go home."

"How are you feeling, sweetheart?" I peek up to see Kathryn in the doorway of my room. I had almost forgotten I was supposed to be resting with a headache.

"Oh, I'm okay. Fran was just checking on me. I'm about to lie down for a few more minutes." Fran eyes me, but I pay her no attention.

"Okay, sweetie. Well, I'll check on you a little bit later," Kathryn promises with a slight wave. "Tomorrow we're going to be taking a trip to a museum, so you need to get your rest while you can." She gracefully glides from the room.

"About to lie back down?" Fran asks.

"I have to call Evie. I haven't checked on her since I've been here," I whisper.

"Oh, okay," she says matching my hushed tone. "Tell Bug, Aunt Fran loves her."

I wave her out the door and collapse onto the bed.

I dial the number cautiously, hoping Evie is the one to answer the phone. To my surprise, she is.

"Hi, Momma! How's Malibu?"

"Why it's just lovely, baby, but I sure am missing you!"

"I miss you too, Momma."

"What have you and Daddy been doing? Have you guys been having fun?"

She lowers her voice. "No. Daddy and Melissa have been fighting a lot."

My first instinct is to be mad that they've been fighting in front of Evie. Then again, I'm curious about what they've been fighting about.

"Well, baby, if they start arguing again, you just go to your room and turn up your radio so you can't hear, okay?"

"Yes ma'am. Oh, Momma, Daddy wants to talk to you!"

"Oh, honey, I don't have time..."

"Here, Daddy!" I hear her yell. Oh, no. This is just what I don't need right now. As if my day hasn't been hard enough.

"Quinn?"

"Yeah, Spencer. What do you need?"

"I, uh, I just wanted to talk to you."

"Have you and Melissa been fighting in front of Evie?"

"No. Well, not actual fighting. Just a couple of heated arguments. She's gone now."

"What do you mean she's gone?"

"I mean, I told her I wanted my wife back. Quinn, I know it'll take time, but I'm going to prove to you that I'm a changed man. I made a terrible mistake, and I need you to forgive me."

My whole world has come crashing down around me. I

went from being a married mother with best friends to a single mother trapped in a nightmare. I have two guys professing their love to me. One I don't want to be with and the other I want to be with for our child's sake, but I'm not sure I can trust him.

I could do it. Easily. I could pack my things and tell Fran we're leaving. Tell his family that there's been an emergency and we have to catch the first plane out.

I wouldn't need to hold up my end of the bargain anymore because I wouldn't need Brett's end of the bargain. My instinct is to forgive this man and think of my daughter, but I just can't seem to spit out the words 'I forgive you.'

"I can't think about this right now, Spencer." I'm a woman of my word and I *will* finish this week in one piece. Brett is a wonderful guy, even if I'm not in love with him, and I can't leave him high and dry after he's been all but taking care of me and dealing with my mess for the last two weeks.

"I know. I'm not rushing you. I'll wait for as long as I need to. You're worth it."

"I have to go, Spencer. Tell Evie I'll be home in a few days." I hang up the phone before anyone else has a chance to proclaim their love for me. The headache I was once faking has now festered into the real deal. I rub my head and turn on my side.

I can't help it. I *do* love Spencer. I've loved him since I was a just a kid. He practically raised me. How am I supposed to shrug him off?

I'm not sure I can do that. I'm sure of one thing though. I'm no longer having fun. That's something that needs to be remedied.

Despite my headache, I quickly put on my bathing suit and make my way outside to where the others are. Phil and Brett are in the water now as Fran lies out on a towel, and Nell is still furiously building her sand castle with the help of Kathryn and Joe.

"Feeling better, dear?" Kathryn asks as I arrive.

"Yes, ma'am. I suppose I'm just not used to so much fun in the sun," I say with a weak smile.

As I walk out into the water with the guys I hear Brett tell Phil, "I'll catch you later," and he quickly swims back to shore.

"How's the headache?" Brett asks.

"All better," I say, reaching for his body and pulling him close. I turn to put my back against his stomach, and I playfully rub myself against him.

"What are you doing?" he chuckles.

I turn to face him, putting my arms around his neck. "Having fun."

He shakes his head. "Not here. Nell is right on the beach."

"Brett, we're chest-high in water. No one will see a thing, I promise."

"Quinn, no," he says sternly, removing my hands from around his neck. I let them fall onto the top of the water.

"What's wrong?" I ask, my brows pushing together in confusion.

He wipes his face with a wet hand. "I just can't right now."

What does he mean he 'can't'? Does he mean physically? Or does he mean because his family is so close?

"Honestly, Brett. Where's your sense of adventure?"

"I just can't right now. Okay?" His voice is pleading, and he sounds almost desperate for me to understand. I nod quickly. He swims back to shore, and I'm left alone, floating in my own confusion.

Tonight, like last night, we lie in dead silence. He's turned on his side facing away from me, and I wonder if that's on purpose. So, I cuddle up to him tonight, spooning him, running my hand slowly down his bare chest.

He moves my hand and turns to lie on his back. "What are you doing, now?"

Is he serious? "I want to make love."

"You want sex after I already said no?" He shakes his head. "I'll never understand you, Quinn. One minute you're hot, the next you're cold. One minute you're game, the next you're not. One minute you're my friend, the next you can take me or leave me."

"What's going on with you today, Brett?" I ask, shaking my head at his brutal honesty.

"Call it a sudden case of whiplash. You keep changing the rules on me. Did you have a headache today, Quinn? Did you?"

I bow my head, suddenly ashamed.

"See, you didn't hold up your end of the bargain today, Quinn." He removes my hand from his lower stomach again and turns back on his side, putting his back to me again, which I think is a little childish, though I don't say so.

I lie softly back onto my pillow from my half-up position and think about what he said. I suppose I have been treating him like a yo-yo. Something to play with. He's even right about my not holding up my end of the bargain today.

I guess he knew I was faking all along. I close my eyes, wanting to cry and feeling more than a little embarrassed and rejected—a feeling I've come to know all too well due to Spencer. Yet I lie here missing him and mad at Brett. Where are you, brain?

15

BRETT

WELL, I fouled up this time. She's in the bathroom putting her war paint on, and I'm hearing sniffle after sniffle. I've knocked on the door a few times to check on her, but all she's been saying is she'll be out in five minutes... for the past hour now. I don't know what came over me yesterday. I usually have such a long fuse. I wasn't angry per say, but I was feeling a little cheap.

I bet even Phil would feel a little bit sleazy if he were in my shoes. I just wasn't in the mood for games, and I used her headache as an excuse to get out of sex yet again. I'm sick of this feeling.

Or maybe I'm just tired of feeling taken advantage of. I know Phil is right, and I've fallen for her. I also know Fran is right, and I can't keep putting myself out there to get hurt. So where does that leave me?

I'm just a puppet in her world of rules, and the fact that she makes them up as she goes along doesn't help my anger any. I haven't made my deal up as I've gone along. She moves me around like I'm a piece in her twisted game of chess, and I'm tired of it.

But I must admit that I'm sorry I hurt her. All it did was complicate things further.

Sniff. Sniff.

"You okay in there, Quinn?"

"I'm fine. I'll be ready in—"

"Five minutes," I interrupt.

Sniff. Sniff.

I roll my eyes at my own stupidity. "Quinn," I say through the door between us, "I'm sorry about last night, I—"

"It's fine." *Sniff.* "I understand." *Sniff.*

I rub the top of my head — a nervous habit I picked up when I was young. It seems to sooth me somehow, yet today it falls short.

She finally opens the door, and I can see why it took her so long to get ready. Her eyes are red, as is her nose, and she has a tissue in her hand, blotting the mascara under her eyes. She obviously kept crying off her makeup.

"C'mere," I say, holding out my arms. "Don't cry. It was just me being a jerk." She cautiously enters my arms, and I squeeze her tight. "Don't cry, Quinn."

"No, you were completely right last night. Everything you said was justified. You didn't make me cry. My own selfishness did."

I set her body away from mine to stare into her eyes, but I hold her by her arms. "Quinn, I don't think you're selfish. You came here to help me, so I know you're not. You could have said no, but you didn't. That being said, I do think you're confused. Who wouldn't be after a divorce? I know I am!"

"I am confused," she admits.

"I know, but I've said it before, and I'll say it again — I'm not something you will have to survive. My tongue gets away from me now and again, like anyone's, I suspect, but I'm here for you, and I'll be anything you need me to be—lover, friend, or more if you'd let me."

Her eyes, which had been staring down, now shoot up to me. "More?"

"Don't take that the wrong way. I'm not pushing you into anything, and I'm not saying we should be engaged like we're pretending to be, but yeah, I want to take care of you. I shouldn't have let my mouth run away from me last night."

She nods and takes a step back, sniffling one last time and tossing her tissue onto the dresser. "I'm ready to go now. We shouldn't keep your family waiting any longer."

I nod. "Okay."

———

AT THE ART MUSEUM, we go our separate ways. Surprisingly, Fran sticks by my side, and Phil goes with Quinn. I imagine Phil is trying to get whatever scoop he can on Fran, and Fran is trying to avoid Phil. I chuckle at the thought.

"Make any progress with her?" Fran asks.

"For about five minutes before I inevitably screwed it up."

She shakes her head at my admission. "What is it with you men?"

"We men? What is it with women?"

"Oh, don't lump me in with Miss Out-of-her-mind over there. I don't understand her either."

"Have you talked to her?" I ask.

"Tried to. Didn't get far."

I take her by the arm and lightly drag her to the farthest corner away from Quinn. "What's the story here? She gets divorced and loses her grip on reality or what?"

"No, no. Nothing like that. Actually, she was doing quite

well, until..." Her voice trails off.

"Until?"

"Well, let's just say you're not the only man in her life pining over her. Apparently not *nearly* the only one."

"Perfect," I say sarcastically. "I don't make things easy on myself, do I?"

"When has love ever been easy?"

I raise my brows. "You have a point. So, what, I just leave her alone to make a decision?"

"What else can you do?"

"Nothing, I suppose, but I feel awfully stupid about this morning now." I mutter the last sentence under my breath.

"What happened this morning?" she asks, suddenly intrigued.

"I, uh, told her if she wanted to be friends or more, that I wouldn't argue more or less."

"Oh, no."

"Yeah, not the smartest move on my part, I guess."

"Look," she says, suddenly excited. "Who says this has to be a bad thing?"

"What do you mean?"

"Well, now she knows how you feel. If she thought you weren't an option, then she wouldn't give you consideration, but now she knows you are."

"Fran, I'm not a mortgage company. Consideration?"

"Do you love her, or don't you?"

I look away. "I don't want to use the word 'love,' but I certainly have strong feelings for her. Don't ask me how."

"Oh please, you're just one of those guys."

"One of those guys?"

"Yeah, yeah. One of those guys who sees the damsel in distress and wants to rescue her. There's always one of you. Sadly, in your case though, there happens to be three of you."

Three of us? Who else would manage to be wrapped up in all this? Granted she's lovely, but who is available in her life who knows her as well as I have come to know her?

"Who are the other two?"

She glances around and leans in. "Her best friend, Thomas, for starters, but the one you have to worry about is her ex-husband, Spencer."

I whip my head back. "Spencer? The one who did all this to her? Surely she isn't considering..."

"Oh, but I'm afraid she is," she interrupts, and my heart sinks. All I can do is stare down at this small girl before me in disbelief.

"Why?"

She opens her mouth to speak but promptly closes it, and her eyes dart around. "I can't tell you why, but it's a bad reason. In her mind a good one, but it's a bad one, and it would only make things worse."

Why can't she tell me? She's told me *this* much. Why stop now? "You're her friend. Why are you telling me all this?"

"Look, I don't agree with whatever you and Quinn have going on. I think it is foolish, and someone is bound to get hurt." The same words Janine used. "I've seen her with you, and it's the first time a man has made her laugh and feel good since her divorce. I just don't want her throwing that away for her ex, who will only eventually hurt her again."

"What about her friend Thomas?"

Her face twists into a disgusted expression. "Thomas is all fine and good, but I know Quinn, and she would never ruin their friendship that way. It's not going to happen."

I take a deep breath and relax a bit, knowing I'm only up against one man after all. It's a man she has history with though. Not a good history, but women usually go for the guy they're more comfortable with. I spot her over by an abstract painting, and I recognize it immediately. I approach her slowly, taking in her beauty and the adorable, confused look on her face.

"It's called 'Jacqueline au Bandeau de Face,'" I tell her. "Pablo Picasso painted it."

"It looks like a children's painting," she scoffs. "I'll never understand art."

I laugh lightly. "Jacqueline was his second wife. It's said that he courted her while still married to his first wife, bringing her a single rose every day from the day he met her until his first wife died. Shortly after that, he married her. He was quite the womanizer, but he painted Jacqueline more than any other woman. Some two hundred or so paintings, I believe."

"Why do men do that?" she asks, never taking her eyes from the painting.

"Do what?"

"Court other women behind their wife's backs."

"Are you under the impression that some women don't do the same?"

"I don't understand *anyone* who does it."

I shrug. "Neither do I." She peeks up at me.

"So, you've never...?"

"Oh, I played around when I was a teenager, no doubt. Run around on my wife though? Never. Not even in our darkest hours."

She glances back at the painting for a moment. "I don't foresee my buying any of Picasso's work any time soon."

I laugh. "Me neither. The gigolo."

She laughs and rests her cheek on my chest, and I put my arm around her waist. I may have insulted Mr. Picasso, but I was certainly thanking him for his painting right now. It brought a smile back to her face. Picasso might have just brought us a little bit closer.

16

QUINN

HEARING the story Brett told me about the painting gave me a little bit of an insight into the minds of some men. I say 'some' because I don't want to be the sort of woman who thinks all men are pigs. Now we're headed to some seafood restaurant that Brett says is wonderful.

I must admit I'm a little nervous. I've never been much of a seafood person, but I don't want to seem picky or ruin it for everyone else. Fran and Phil seem to be the most excited about it —both being huge fans of lobster—and with Brett paying, I'm sure they will order only the best.

"Are you excited?" Brett asks me.

I shrug a bit. "A little nervous."

He tilts his head. "Nervous?"

"I'm afraid I don't know much about seafood."

"That's nothing to be worried about. I know just what to order you, and I'll have the same."

When we arrive at the restaurant, it's not what I was expecting at all. I was sure we would be going to some fancy five-star restaurant with chandeliers and people tidily patting the corners of their mouths with their napkins, but I was wrong.

There are people laughing and joking, and the hostess seems to know Kathryn and Joe well, as they talk all the way to our table. There are small ceiling fans hanging down, and the interior looks much like a log house. Brett pulls out my chair like the gentleman he is, and Phil does the same for Fran. I glance over the menu and see all sorts of seafood delights, and I peek around at other tables to see what everyone else is eating and if it appeals to me.

"You won't be needing this," Brett says, taking the menu from my hands. Relief washes over me, knowing that he plans to order for me. It's times like this I realize how different we are. I grew up on fried chicken and cheeseburgers while he grew up on lobster and caviar.

I sink into my seat just a little as I see Kathryn and Joe looking over their menus and discussing what they intend to order. Boy, do I feel out of place, but as I stare at Kathryn and Joe, I start to wonder what it would be like in their relationship with yearly trips and lobster dinners.

It's not just that. They seem to have fun together. It's not about the money for them. They're not the kind of snobby people who think of money first. They didn't even blink when their son offered to pay for three extra people to accompany them on this trip.

Brett takes great pleasure in ordering us crab legs while Phil and Joe order lobster to share with Fran and Kathryn. Anne and Russ, on the other hand, order steaks and get Nell crab cakes, which she's excited about. Even the child knows more about seafood than I do.

"Crab? Isn't that going to kind of break the bank?" I whisper to Brett.

"Not even close. I'm just starting you out with something a bit simpler. Next time we'll get the lobster," he says in my ear.

"No whispering at the table," huffs Phil.

"Yeah, love birds," Anne says with a smile.

"Oh, come now, I'm just wooing my beautiful bride," says Brett, and I shudder slightly at the word "bride."

"I think it's adorable," says Kathryn. "Don't you think it's adorable, Joe?"

"Yeah, adorable," he says nonchalantly, taking a bite of buttered roll.

I glance to Fran who offers me a consoling smile.

What seems like an hour later, our food arrives, and I'm dumbstruck when my plate is placed in front of me. I grab Brett's leg under the table. "It's actually *legs*," I say to him in hushed tone.

He chuckles softly. "Hence the phrase 'crab legs.' Don't worry. Here, I'll show you how it's done." He takes a leg in his left hand and what looks like a nut cracker in his right.

"This is your crab cracker," he says, holding up the oversized nutcracker. "You see where the joints are on the legs? You turn the leg sideways and simply crack it with the cracker," he explains as he demonstrates. "You see the way it breaks? Now you pull it apart, and the meat will come out."

A small piece of meat escapes from the leg as he pulls it apart. "Then, take your long-stemmed fork, pierce the meat, and dip it in the butter sauce." He takes his bite and winks at me as he chews. "Now you try."

I mimic his actions, and soon I'm rewarded with my own small piece of meat. "This seems like a lot of work for such a small piece of meat," I say to him as the others are now immersed in their own individual conversations.

"Oh, but you haven't tried the meat yet. It's well worth it. Go on, dip it in the sauce."

I dip the small piece of meat from my fork into the sauce and smell it before placing it in my mouth. The taste is overwhelmingly buttery and sweet all at once.

"It's delightful. Completely wonderful," I say, eager to crack the next joint of the leg.

"I knew you would like it."

I thought I knew everything about men. I thought I knew their overall tendencies and behaviors, but Brett shows me something different. Something fun.

He brings out a fun side in me. It's obviously not sex—though I have to admit, sometimes I wish it were—it's the care-free manner in which he lives his life. Taking me up on my original offer shows me that alone.

We've had our ups and downs during this time, but I can recognize my own faults. They were my fault. He's done all he can do to make me feel welcome and part of the family, and I sometimes forget that it's all a sham because he's not mine.

———

"WHAT ARE YOU THINKING ABOUT?" he asks as we lie in bed tonight.

"Everything." Truth.

"Can I ask you something?"

"Shoot."

He turns over on his side to face me. "What was life like with Spencer before..." His voice trails off.

I roll onto my side now to meet his eyes. "Truthfully?" He nods. "Mundane. Every day was the same. Wake up, go to work, come home and eat, go to sleep." I intentionally leave out helping my child with school work and taking care of her.

"What about with you and Lisa? How was life with her before you married her?" My voice a mere whisper.

His brows twitch. "Some days were good. Other days were bad. Just like any other relationship, I assume. I thought if I married her, things would get better. She always pushed for marriage."

"Do you think she ever loved you?"

He shakes his head ever so slightly. "No. I don't think she's capable of love." He takes a breath. "What about Spencer? You think he loved you?"

"I think so. I think he just saw someone younger who was intrigued by him, and he with her and..."

"Yeah," he says, knowing I can't put it into words. "What's she like? This other woman?"

I scowl. "You'll laugh."

"I won't," he promises, crossing his heart with his hand then holding up three fingers. "Scout's honor."

I chuckle. "She was a stripper. I didn't even know Spencer went to places like that. Apparently, he had been frequenting her place for quite some time after we moved to the city. I guess they became infatuated with one another.

"She saw an older man with money who could take care of her, and he saw a young woman with a nice body that could give him pleasure and make him feel like a kid again. However, I don't think it will last between them."

"Why do you say that?"

I shrug. "Because that's not who they truly are. A woman isn't defined by her job or her body, and a man isn't defined by his money. If they think of one another like that, then they are both in for a rude awakening, if there hasn't been one already."

He lowers his eyes until they appear almost closed.

"What's wrong?"

"I know I told you I wasn't going to push you into anything you weren't ready for," he begins, "but we have to be on the same page right now."

I nod. "Go on."

His chest rises, and I can tell something important is on his mind.

"I want us to be friends."

I sit up on my elbow. "Are we not already?"

He sits up now, too. "I don't know," he laughs, "are we?"

"Well, I certainly thought we were. I wouldn't be sharing all this with you if I didn't consider you my friend."

"Well, Quinn, I have to admit that sometimes you throw me for a loop. There are times, like tonight at dinner and right now while you're confiding in me, that I think we are, but there's other times when I feel like you'd rather I wasn't around at all."

I rest my head in my hand. "I suppose you're right."

"I know you have a lot on your mind."

"I do."

"I know, and I fancy myself an understanding man, but you have to throw me a bone here. One day you didn't come out of your room until almost sunset, then you just jumped in the water wanting sex right then and there. Even a man has to warm up to the idea first," he laughs.

I let out a chuckle through my nose. "That was kind of silly of me, I guess. I just thought it might be a little erotic with an audience."

He chuckles. "Well, it would have been different for sure. Look, I don't want to change who you are. I love who you are. I've never met anyone like you, but if we're going to be lovers, and you're going to be pretend to be my fiancé, there can't be this oddness between us.

"I have to be able to come to you and you to me. If we can be friends, then the rest of this week will be a cake walk, I promise. My family already loves you. We just have to get through these last three days. Deal?"

"Deal."

17

BRETT

"I WANT to do something nice for her," I tell Fran and Phil, sipping my coffee at the kitchen table while Quinn still sleeps.

"Why? Because it went over so well the first time?" Phil asks.

"Phil," I say in annoyance.

"Brett, it's not often I side with Phil, but I have to agree. I thought you and I talked about this. You were going to stop pushing her right now."

"We did, I know, but this isn't going to be like the bath incident. We made progress last night."

Phil's eyes light up. "A whirl and twirl under the sheets yet?" he says, wiggling his brows.

"Phil, have you no filter at all?"

"Or class," Fran says with a slap to his arm.

"Well, go on then, what kind of progress?" he asks with a roll of his eyes.

"Just progress. A friendship. That's all."

"She finally opened up to you?" Fran asks, wide-eyed.

I nod excitedly, probably seeming like a giddy school girl,

but I promptly clear my throat as roughly as possible. "So, tell me, what can I do for her? What does she like?"

"She likes sex, remember?" Phil says loudly.

"Phil!" Fran and I yell in hushed tones. He puts his hands up as if surrendering.

"Well, she loves animals, but I wouldn't suggest buying her a dog," she laughs.

"Get her a stuffed bear," Phil says with an annoyed wave of his hand, tired of this mundane conversation Fran and I are sharing.

"You'd do better with a stuffed giraffe," Fran mumbles over her coffee.

"What does that mean?" I ask.

She shrugs. "She's just always had a thing for giraffes."

My eyes widen, and I'm sure they glisten and twinkle like Kris Kringle's. If she wants a giraffe, I'll give her one. Well, I won't give her one obviously, but I can take her to them.

"There's a zoo in Los Angeles. It would be an hour drive but maybe worth it."

"Oh, that'd be perfect!" Fran says with a clap of her hands.

"I don't want her to think of it as a date," I say with a sigh, nibbling my lip.

"Then take Nell with you," she suggests.

"Hey, that's a great idea. I'm going to go get her up so she can get dressed and ready. Don't tell her where I'm taking her. Let it be a surprise."

I dash up the stairs moments later, having poured her a cup of coffee. When I make it to our room, I almost hate to wake her. This is by far the most beautiful I've ever seen her.

Don't get me wrong, she's gorgeous when she's awake, and no, I'm not one of those men who think it's all cute when a girl first wakes up. It's just that she finally seems at peace now. She appears comfortable and relaxed, and a part of me can't wait to watch her eyes slowly open, half lid, half eye, groggy with messy hair. Okay, maybe I *am* one of those guys.

I wave the cup of coffee under her nose and let her breathe in the aroma. Then her bright green eyes appear from behind her lids.

"Good morning," I softly say as she sits up in bed.

"Room service. It *is* a good morning." She takes the cup from me and wraps her hands around the hot mug as if to warm them.

"Care to go on an adventure today?"

She cocks her head and eyes me. "I'm not sure I can handle any more adventures."

I chuckle. "Well, I think this one you'll enjoy. Get up, get dressed, and put on some comfortable shoes. I'll be waiting downstairs with Nell."

"With Nell?"

"Yeah, I'm going to see if she wants to be your chaperone. I can't take a lady out without a chaperone. What would people say?"

"Okay then. I'll be down in a little bit."

I can't resist placing my bum on the stair banister and sliding down it, wobbling the whole way. When my feet hit the floor, I clap loudly and fight the urge to let out a "yee-haw," though I've never been to the South.

"I take it she's going," Fran chuckles with a wink.

"So far, so good," I say.

I speak with Anne, and she loves the idea of Quinn and me taking Nell to the zoo. She gets Nell ready, packing her a backpack of juice pouches and some cash in case she sees something she wants. I try to assure her they have juice at the zoo, but you can't tell my sister anything.

Russ is excited to know that he and Anne will get a child-free day at the beach and maybe a little rumble under the covers. I suppose while the cat is away, the mice will play. I'm happy to be her babysitter for the day. There's nothing on this planet I love more than my niece. It makes me eager to have children of my own one day.

Lisa and I talked about children, but the talk was brief. I wanted children, and she didn't. She told me if she had a baby then *she* would no longer be the baby. Spoiled till the end, she was. I want loads of children, a bushel of them.

I can't wait until the day I come home and three or four kids storm the door aching for a hug or a ride on my shoulders. Lisa never could understand it. She thought of the sticky fingers fouling up her freshly waxed car and the bedrooms full of toys rather than her pretty little things like bags and shoes. While we were married, our spare bedrooms were filled to the brim with the ridiculousness. I'm glad those days are over.

Though I'm not jaded like Quinn seems to be. She didn't have the happy childhood I had either. I had parents to show me what true love and companionship was. Which is why I knew when it was time to file for divorce.

Quinn came from a home where her dad was unfaithful and abandoned her. Then she married, only for history to repeat itself like it always seems to do. My heart aches for her at the thought of it. Every time I sense that she's hurting, it chips a small piece of my heart away. Is that love? It's been so long since I've felt it that I'm not sure.

Nell sits in the backseat, legs swinging to and fro, peering from window to window in excitement. I glance at Quinn's hands placed delicately in her lap and wonder, would it be a crime to hold her hand in her opinion? Just as quick as I think it, her eyes meet mine and she follows my gaze to her hands.

I promptly avert my eyes back to the road, but then she removes my right hand from the wheel and intertwines her fingers in mine. I fight a smile and hope I don't look as surprised as I am. She simply stares out her window and rubs my hand with her thumb. A small victory.

————

WHEN WE ARRIVE at the zoo, Nell is jumping around, back-pack in tow, and holding my and Quinn's hands, having us swing her in the air on every count of three. Quinn's smile broadens my own.

Nell is small for her age, having been born a bit premature, but there's a whole lot of fire inside that brown-haired beauty. She reminds me so much of Anne at that age, and for being only six, she is extremely smart and tends to pick up on grown up feelings easily.

"Oh, look, Uncle Brett! Monkeys!" she yells, letting our hands fall and running toward the chimps. It goes like that the whole day. Nell sees all the beautiful creatures, and Quinn follows by my side, smiling. We stop at the snow cone bar before I pull the trick from up my sleeve.

"You have to get a rainbow snow cone, Aunt Quinn. Everyone knows that," Nell lectures before ordering one for each of us. Quinn glances to me with slightly pursed lips, as if she's not sure it's okay that she be referred to as "Aunt Quinn." I'm not so sure either. I offer her a smile and shrug to hopefully put her mind at ease.

Once we have our snow cones, I take Quinn by the hand and lead her to where the giraffes are. Her eyes light up, and her mouth gapes open.

"I didn't think they had giraffes. I thought we were heading home."

"No, no. This is just the main event," I tell her with a squeeze of her hand. "I couldn't let you come all this way without seeing what you love most."

Her head jerks toward me with narrowed eyes. "How did you know I liked giraffes?"

"Um... you talk in your sleep?" I laugh.

She nudges me with her elbow. "About giraffes?"

I laugh. "I can't help it if your subconscious likes giraffes."

She giggles. "Uh huh."

"I like giraffes, too, Aunt Quinn!"

"You do?" she laughs, picking Nell up into a hug. "Well, it's a good thing Uncle Brett brought us here then, isn't it?" Nell giggles away and wraps her arms around Quinn's neck.

When we arrive home, Nell jumps into Russ's arms and tells him and Anne all about her trip with Uncle Brett and Aunt Quinn. Quinn heads upstairs, and I follow. She sits on the bed and begins to remove her shoes.

"I wouldn't get too comfortable if I were you," I tell her.

"Oh yeah? Why is that?"

"Because we have a road trip to go on for dinner. The adventure has just begun."

18

QUINN

"WHERE ARE WE?" I ask, having ridden with Brett almost three hours from Malibu.

"This is the Palm Springs Aerial Tramway," Brett says as we step inside an aerial car held up by only wires.

"*This* is the adventure? Seems more like a gamble, if you ask me." I hold onto one of the inside bars. The glass box he has me in is completely empty save us and one chaperone. "We're the only ones going up?"

"Usually there are more, but I know a guy."

"He knows a guy," I mumble to myself, still gripping the silver bar for all it's worth. "How far are we going up?"

"Some eight-thousand feet. It'll take us about ten minutes to get to our destination."

"Where is that?"

"Dinner."

"All this for dinner?"

"Of course. They have the best food in town. Now let go of the bar and enjoy the ride," he laughs, putting his arms around me as I lean my back against him.

I hate to admit it, but it feels nice just to be held by someone. It feels even nicer to go on a little adventure and be wined and dined. It's been forever since someone has gone out of his way for me.

I watch in amazement as we climb at a crawling speed and hover over cliffs where sprouts of green bushes invade the rock. I let Brett's arms fall from around me and I walk to the edge of the car, placing my hands against the glass and peering down below us.

"This is amazing," I whisper to myself. I glance to my left and right to see we are surrounded by bedrock and my usual squeamish nature of heights fades away into wonder and giddiness.

"Yes, it is," he says, as if seeing it for the first time.

"Hold on, guys," the young, female chaperone says, "another car is coming down."

"Why do we have to hold on for that?" I ask Brett.

He chuckles. "You'll see."

At once the car passes us and our car begins to rock back and forth. "Whoaaa," I say as I giggle and try to keep my feet planted beneath me. Brett holds on to my waist and now both my hands grip the silver bar. Even the girl laughs at my giddiness, though she hides it under her hand.

I peek behind us, walking to the back end of the car. Below us, I see what looks like a small town. "Is that Palm Springs down there?"

Brett laughs. "Yup. That's it alright."

"Oh my, this is beautiful."

We finally arrive at the restaurant some ten minutes later, and I'm surprised when I'm told we traveled just over two miles. Brett orders our food and two glasses of wine. We sit right next to the window where we can see all the way down to the city. It's glorious. I shake my head.

"What's that for?" he asks.

"Do you do this for all your friends?"

"Sure I do."

"Uh huh. So why aren't Phil and Fran here with us then?"

He closes his eyes for a moment and gives a sarcastic shrug. "They didn't want to come."

I know he's lying, but this is one lie that I enjoy and let pass. It washes over me like the mountain air. The waiter brings our wine, and before I can take a sip, Brett raises his glass.

"Let's toast," he says.

"Okay." I hold mine up as well. "What are we toasting?"

"To our friendship. May it always be as beautiful as this."

I blush slightly, feeling the blood rush to my cheeks, but I tap his glass with mine and take a sip to our toast.

A short time later, they are serving our food, and I have to admit it is pretty good. I remember thinking in the aerial car that this was a lot of trouble to go through for a meal, but I realize now that it's the experience that makes it worthwhile. It's not just the ride, though that was spectacular, and it's not just the food, though it is good. It's everything put together. Not to mention his finding out my weak spot for giraffes.

He has obviously put a lot of thought into today, which is a lot more than I could have ever said for Spencer. Thomas might have tried to do something similar, but he probably would have tripped over his own toes to get it done. Brett's execution is perfect.

He knew I'd feel more comfortable today if Nell was with us. He waited until the end of the trip to take me to the giraffes because he knew I could spend all the time I wanted there if we saw them last. He knew I'd find the aerial car exhilarating, and he knew I'd love this restaurant, which seems to sit upon a mountain, staring down at the world.

This day is the first time since I've been here that I've smiled all day. None were forced or because I was playing the role of dutiful fiancé. They were all genuine. I see now that I could have had this all along, had I just given Brett a proper chance. I won't make that mistake again.

The ride home is glorious. We ride the tramway back down, and I am absolutely giddy. By the time we make it home, Fran and Phil are the only ones awake. They are probably waiting up for us, if I know Fran at all.

"Thank you for today. It was... perfect." I kiss him on the cheek, and now he's the one blushing. I head up the stairs with Fran, who is now pulling me away from him.

"What is it?" I ask her. "What's the hurry?"

"Details! Details!" she yells, pulling me into her room. "You've left me alone all day with *Phil*, which we will talk about later. The least you can do is give me details."

"You're the one who told him I love giraffes, aren't you? No one else could have told him, and there's no other way he could have known."

She kicks at imaginary dirt. "It might've slipped out during our conversation."

"What conversation? Why are you even talking to him about me?" I laugh.

"Well, what am I supposed to do? Sit back while you waste your life away thinking of that loser, Spencer, and pushing the perfect guy away?"

My head snaps back. "That's how you feel?"

"Oh, Quinn. If you can stand there and tell me you feel nothing for that guy, then I'll never interfere again."

I stare into her eyes for a moment before my eyes find the floor, and now *I'm* wishing there were dirt to kick.

"Can you tell me that? Can you tell me you feel nothing for him?"

I suck in a breath of air. "No, I can't say that. Not after tonight."

She pulls me onto the bed, and we lie on our backs staring up at the ceiling, gossiping just like kids. "Tell me everything," she says. "Spill!"

"Well, we took Nell to the zoo, as you know. Then he took me to the Aerial Tramway, and we rode the car up to this restaurant where we had dinner and wine. That's all."

She sits up on her elbow. "That's *all*?"

"Well, I wouldn't say it like that. I mean, there were times when he'd hold me around my waist or arms. There was a time when the aerial car started swaying, and that was a lot of fun. He saved the giraffes for last at the zoo, so I could admire them longer. We toasted to our new friendship over wine."

"Your new friendship? I don't know about you, but I don't have friends like that."

"Like what?"

"Who hold me and take me places to see amazing things and take me on rides through the mountains. Actually, come to think of it, I've never even had a boyfriend who did those things."

I chuckle. "It *was* pretty amazing."

She grabs my hand. "You could have it all the time, you know. Look, I've talked to Brett, and I know you better than you know yourself. You need to give this guy a real chance."

I sink down further into the bed. "I feel that way sometimes, too, but how can I? How can I, after lying to his family this whole time and being the 'I only want sex' girl?

"You can. And Phil... well..."

My head jerks toward her. "No. You and... seriously?"

"We didn't have sex, if that's what you're thinking, but you can't just leave me alone with him for days on end and expect nothing to happen."

"Oh, no."

She laughs. "Believe it or not, underneath all the gold chains and swimsuit stunts, he's a good guy. He's been, well, courting me."

"Tell, tell." Now I'm the one staring down at her.

"We've just done a little making out here and there. A little teasing in the water at night. Tonight, we just laid on the couch together while you guys were out, and we talked about our jobs and the kind of people we've dated. I talked a lot about you, and he talked about Brett. He even mentioned how perfect it would be if you guys were a couple and we were a couple, too. Talked about all the wonderful double dates we could take to Yankees games or going out to eat and maybe come back here next year with the family."

"Well, you guys just sat around and mapped out our whole lives, didn't you?"

She giggles. "No, but it would be pretty great. We all get along. Brett is perfect for you, and I've seen a side of Phil that I could get used to."

I clap her leg. "Well, I'm happy for you, Fran. You deserve it."

"What about you?"

I smile. "I'm starting to think I deserve it, too."

19

BRETT

I'VE FINALLY MADE PROGRESS; I'm no longer walking on eggshells around Quinn. I've seen a carefree side to her that I hadn't witnessed before. She's opening up slowly, blossoming. I find myself hating her ex-husband, Spencer, for what he did to her, and I hope I have showed her during the past two days that she can have a life without him—a happy life.

I didn't set out yesterday to romance her, but I suppose that's what happened. I only wanted to show her a lovely day and hopefully bring her out of her shell. She finally opened up. It just took a little bit of understanding and a six-year-old chaperone. I chuckle to myself.

"What do we have here?" I ask as I walk into the living area and see Phil with his arm around Fran as they drink their morning coffee.

"What can I say? He's starting to grow on me," Fran says, nudging Phil.

"It was only a matter of time. No woman can resist me forever," Phil says, his chin held to the sky.

Fran rolls her eyes as I do, and I fix a cup of coffee and sit with them.

"Quinn still asleep?" he asks.

"Yeah, she's tuckered out from yesterday, I imagine."

"I had a long talk with her when ya'll got back," Fran sings into her coffee.

"Oh, is that so?" I ask. "What was said?"

She shrugs. "Just girl talk. She told me what a wonderful time she had is all."

I can imagine it now. The two of them whispering in Fran's room last night. Quinn telling Fran all about our romantic night. Although it wasn't meant to be romantic, I'm glad it turned out that way.

Some might call me a liar, but I truly was only trying to be a good friend and tear her away from all her worries and troubles. Hopefully that's what I did, and if I did a little more than that, so be it. I would love nothing more than to be a part of her life forever, even in the smallest of ways.

"So, what are we going to do today?" Phil asks.

Fran shrugs. "I don't know. As much as I love the beach, I'm getting a little burned out on it. Five days in a row of laying out and swimming has taken it out of me."

"Quinn said you work with her, that you're her assistant coach," I say.

"That's right."

"Why don't we have ourselves a little game today?"

"Oh my. Quinn would love that."

"Sure," Phil says, "we can let the girls hang out here, and you and I could go to a sporting goods store and pick up a few things."

"You think your mom and dad would play, too?" she asks.

"Sure. My dad loves sports, and my mom will think it's fun. She'd do anything to see Quinn happy anyway."

She claps her hands. "Well, let's do it."

Phil and I leave for the sporting goods store, and my father tags along. It's been a while since I've had a good visit with my dad, so I welcome the time with him. Phil heads to the back of the store while Dad and I check out the gloves.

"This is a wonderful thing you're doing, son. I think Quinn will enjoy it."

"I hope so."

"Son, is it just me, or is Quinn going through a tough time right now?" My dad may not say much, but he sees everything.

"She is. I think it's problems with her ex-husband. He's wanting her back, and it's got her mind all fuzzy."

"Hmm," he moans, staring down at the glove on his hand.

"What is it, Dad?"

"I think sometimes you, your sister, and your mother mistake my quietness for ignorance."

"Dad, I would never think—"

He holds up a hand to silence me. "I know there is more going on with you and Quinn than we know. I know the kind of pressure your mother has put on you since your divorce to start dating. I tried to tell her she was pushing you, but you know your mother. She thinks she knows what's best for us all.

"I know something about your and Quinn's relationship is off. If Quinn is still worried about her ex-husband, then I say postpone getting married and give the girl time to breathe. I assume if her ex-husband is still lingering, then she hasn't been divorced for long. She might need time, and trust me when I say, rushing a woman will get you nowhere but hurt." He peeks over my shoulder, and I turn to see Phil heading our way with a handful of bats. "That's all I'm going to say."

And here, all this time, I thought it was Anne I had to worry about being suspicious. I never thought my father was ignorant. I just thought he didn't pay close attention. I can see now that I was wrong. He said he knows something is off with Quinn and me. I know he won't say anything to the others, but this is the first time since we arrived that I'm worried about my family getting hurt by this whole thing.

I wonder how much he actually knows. Being a man of few words, he probably didn't speak half as many as he thought. I wonder if he knows this is all a sham, but that I've fallen for her, too. I could take what he said so many different ways. That small conversation may have just ruined me.

———

"WHERE HAVE YOU BOYS BEEN?" Quinn asks as we enter the house.

I hold up a bag of gloves. "Sporting goods shopping."

She peeks inside. "Softball gloves."

"Yeah, and we got some bats, too," Phil says, holding up another sack with bats clanking together.

"Dad has one full of yellow softballs," I tell her.

"What's going on?"

"Didn't Fran tell you?" I ask, peeking around her at Fran.

"I thought she'd like the surprise," Fran says.

"We're going to have a softball game today. Right here in the back of the house."

She giggles. "Right here?"

"Yup. We're going to pick teams and make a day of it. You and Fran will be the coaches. We just have to figure out who can be the umpire."

"I think I have someone in mind," Quinn offers.

———

WE PLACE old pillows as bases and anchor them to the ground, first base all the way to home plate. Fran and Quinn agree to be the coaches, and they meticulously pick their players. I'm on Fran's team along with Dad and Anne. Russ, Mom, and Phil are on Quinn's, and she was right. She picked the perfect umpire: Nell.

I smile as I watch her explain to Nell what she needs to do, and I laugh out loud at Mom's first time at bat. Quinn literally has to stand behind my mom, holding the bat with her, to hit the ball. When she finally connects with the ball, my mom is jumping up in the air and squealing as we all yell for her to run.

Phil, on the other hand, fancying himself the next Babe Ruth, thumps the pillow plate with his bat a few times and then calls his shot to center field. The execution is somewhat different though. It heads to short stop where I'm standing, and I easily throw it to Anne at second who tries for the double play by tagging our mother out, but Phil is too quick to first base.

As Russ comes to the plate, Anne jokingly tells everyone to move in, and with that, Russ points the bat at her and tells her to get ready. I watch her stick out her tongue at him right as he makes contact, and the ball heads hard and fast right to her and escapes through her legs into the makeshift outfield where no one is playing. Anne chases after it, as Phil rounds third and goes straight for home, and I hear Nell call out "Safe!" as he slides in, while Anne throws the ball to me and Russ holds his place at third base.

"No more taunting the batters, Anne," Dad jokes, and Anne sticks out her tongue.

When Quinn gets up to bat, she winks at me and I laugh, knowing she's going to hit it right for me, and she doesn't disappoint. It goes straight to me, and I'm able to tag Russ out before throwing the ball to Anne who is covering first. Three outs.

After our turn at bat, we stop keeping score and just let everyone hit and run. I've never seen my mother so excited, and Nell feels important knowing her position is the most crucial. She loves calling people out who are safe and calling people safe whom she knows are out. Obviously, someone has paid off the umpire. I chuckle.

By the time the day ends, we are all exhausted and smiling from ear to ear. Another successful day. Phil and I clean up outside, while the girls head in the house to shower.

"You did good, man. I haven't had that much fun in a long time."

"I haven't either. I think this is the most fun I've ever had here."

"I realize I never properly thanked you for paying my way and letting me come. Thank you, man," he says with a clap to my back.

"No problem, brother. It was worth it to have you here. So, tell me, what *is* going on with you and Fran?"

"Ah, man. I'm totally in love with that girl."

I jerk my head back. "You? Love?"

"What? Am I incapable?" he laughs.

"Nah, man. I've just never heard you use the L word before."

"I've never felt the L word before, until now."

I pick up the last of the balls and toss them in the bucket. "I'm happy for you, bro."

"What about you?"

"What about me?"

"You think you're in love?"

I rub the back of my neck and top of my head nervously. "I don't know. She has me all messed up — I know that. One minute I think I might be, but the next she has me questioning it."

"Sounds like love to me. Looks like love to me, and if it sounds like a duck and looks like a duck it's probably..."

"A duck?"

"Love."

20

QUINN

I AWAKE FEELING ABSOLUTELY REFRESHED. **Divine,** even. I glance to the table on my right and see a single rose upon a letter next to a steaming cup of coffee. I pick up the rose as I open the letter.

Gone fishing with Dad and Russ. Relax and enjoy your coffee.

Brett

I run the rose under my nose and collapse into the plush bedding, taking a long look around the room. I haven't had a chance to admire it since the first day we arrived, and I remember thinking of it as a museum: sparkling clean and untouchable. Now I think of it more as a home, comfortable and welcoming.

I even smile when I think of Brett. He hasn't attempted to have sex with me at all, yet he leaves me flowers and coffee. He takes me to fancy restaurants and arranges softball games for me. He's the kind of guy I've always dreamed of. Honestly, he's the kind of guy I always wished Spencer would be, though he wasn't.

"Knock, knock!" a cheerful voice says from the door. I lean up to find Anne peeking her head in through the door.

"Hey, come on in."

"I'm sorry. I didn't know you were still sleeping."

"No, it's fine. I was just about to get up," I say, grabbing the coffee and taking a sip.

"Well, good, because it's going to be girls' day out today. The Millers down the way are watching Nell, and Mother and I are going shopping and getting our nails done. We want you to come with us. We've barely gotten to speak. Brett keeps you locked up tight." She laughs.

I chuckle. "He's just being protective, I guess." Lie. "I was just a little worried about meeting everyone, and he promised to stay close by." Lie. I tell more lies these days than truth.

"Well, I promise we don't bite. So, finish your coffee, get dressed, and meet us downstairs," she says with a pat on my leg before gracefully making her way from the room.

I see a lot of Brett in Anne. Not just because they are twins, but because it seems like they both go out of their way to make others feel comfortable.

I finish my coffee and wash my face and put on my makeup. After showering last night, I don't bother doing so again. I curl the bottom of my hair and float down the stairs where Anne and Kathryn are filling their purses and grabbing their cell phones.

"You all ready?" Anne asks.

"Yes, I am."

"You look lovely, dear."

"Thanks, Kathryn."

———

AS WE WALK the streets of Malibu, the conversation I knew

was coming but dreaded and still have no real answers for ensues.

"So, have you and Brett set a date?" Kathryn asks.

"No ma'am. We aren't in too big of a hurry. We are more focused on having fun these days." Lie? Truth? I'm not sure.

"You guys could always have the wedding here in Malibu. I can imagine lights hanging from the trees and white table cloths with lit candles everywhere at dusk," Anne says. "Wouldn't that just be lovely, Mom?"

"Oh, yes. Lovely, dear."

"Of course, I would *have* to throw you a shower. I love doing that. I've thrown so many wedding showers and baby showers that I'm practically a professional. You name the party, and I've done it," Anne says, almost jumping out of her skin.

"Well, of course you can, Anne. I'd be honored to have you throw me one," I say. Truth? Lie? Even I can't tell the difference anymore.

We stop to have our nails done, and Anne sits at the table next to me while Kathryn gets a pedicure across the room.

"I've never seen him so happy before," she says, waving one of her hands dry while the other is getting worked on. "Honestly, I've never seen him go to such lengths as he did yesterday to make someone happy."

"Seriously?" That doesn't sound like him. He seems like the sort to *always* go out of his way.

"Don't get me wrong," she says, "my brother is the most kind-hearted man I know. It's just that so many women have taken advantage of it that I think he has learned not to give so much of himself, but with you, he seems comfortable. Not like when he was with Lisa."

"Tell me about Lisa. Do you think she just wanted to get married for the money? I only ask because Brett said that's what he thinks."

She shrugs one of her shoulders. "I'm not sure. Lisa was always so hard to read. She never let anyone in. It was hard even being nice to her because you could never tell whether she was appreciative or not.

"If I had to come to a conclusion, she wasn't all about the money at first. Brett rarely tells people he comes from money. So, I'd say that she wasn't. She must have loved him at some point.

"But as they always say, money will bring out the worst in people. It's the root of all evil. I don't necessarily believe that. I think what people do *for* and *with* the money is what's evil.

"Lisa was willing to marry for the money and didn't care how she spent it. She denied Brett the chance to have kids because she claimed they cost too much, which only told us that she wanted all the money to go into buying *her* things and not providing for children. It's just as well. She's wasn't the motherly type."

As she speaks, it dawns on me exactly the kind of person she must have been. I had a friend like her once who came right out and said she didn't want babies because *she* would no longer be the baby.

"I saw her around Nell," Anne continued, "and that woman had no maternal instincts whatsoever." She glances to me now. "I see something different in you. The way you are with Nell. You must have experience with children. You care about Nell— you wanted her to go to the zoo with the two of you, and you made her a part of the softball game.

"And I think Brett enjoys that part of you. I think he can see a future with you. I also think the rest of us can see you being a perfect addition to our family. My parents already love you so much, especially Mom."

My heart drops deep into the pit of my soul, and all I feel is guilt over what I'm doing to this family. Here she is pouring her heart and soul out to me, and all I'm doing is playing the role I was paid to play like the common prostitute I am.

Hearing her talk about my motherly instincts has me sick to my stomach. If I were any kind of mother at all, I'd be with my child right now—not with some strange man on a vacation, pretending to be something I'm not and taking advantage of good people for sex's sake. I'm ashamed, and I can feel the vomit rising in my throat.

"Excuse me," I say before jumping up and running to the bathroom.

"Quinn?" Anne calls after me, but I ignore her. I get to the bathroom just in time to lock the door and get sick. Shame has made me physically ill, something I didn't even know was a possibility until now.

I stand once more and place my purse on the counter, digging for a mint. There's a knock on the door.

"In use!" I call out. Another knock. "In use!" I call out once more, but again, another knock. I open the door, ready to shout at someone but see that it's my would-be mother-in-law coming to check on me.

"Are you okay, dear?"

I shake my head trying to clear it. "I'm fine. Sorry. I guess I picked up a stomach bug of some sort." Lie.

"I've paid our tickets," Anne says, having joined us in the doorway.

"I'm so sorry."

"You can't help it if you're sick, dear. Let's get you home."

"No, no. I'm fine now. I think some more walking around will make me feel better."

"Are you sure?" Anne asks, and I nod. "Okay, well, it's probably just the fumes in here anyways. Let's go to the antique mall."

"Oh, that's perfect," I gush, "I love antiques." Truth. Finally.

———

I START to feel a little more like myself, though weak. I'm not sure how much longer I can pull off this charade without screaming from the rooftops that there will be no shower, no wedding, and no children. I've hidden my entire real life, not only from his family, but from him.

He may want a relationship with me, but that could only be because he doesn't know I come as a package deal. The more I think about this, the more I miss Evie. I wonder what she's doing now. I wonder if Melissa has come back around. Maybe she has, and maybe she has taken Evie to that movie she asked about less than two weeks ago.

Has it only been two weeks? It seems like ages ago that I met Brett and pulled that little drunken stunt in the Italian place that has now landed me in Malibu, telling more lies. Fran was right in the beginning when she said I wouldn't be able to pull this off without someone getting attached or hurt.

Sooner or later, they will either know the truth, or Brett will tell them we broke up, or I'll tell them. Either way, I can't do this anymore. It hurts too much, and I miss my family.

As the antique stores begin to close up shop and the sun gets lower in the sky, Kathryn decides it's time for us to go home and meet the boys, and I'm all too ready for it.

I woke up today feeling too loved, with fresh-made coffee and a rose upon my table with a note telling me to rest, but there has been no rest today. I know what I'm about to do. I'm about to break his heart, but I can't help it anymore.

One of us will be hurt. There's no way around it. I leave and hurt him, or I tell him that I have a daughter, and he tells me to take a hike for lying to him. Even *I* would tell me to take a hike.

How could I have hidden my child? More importantly, how could I have done this to my child? I shudder.

"You go upstairs and rest, dear," says Kathryn. "I'll be up in a minute with a warm cup of tea for you. I'm sure the boys will be here soon."

"Yes ma'am," I say, climbing the stairs for probably the last time. I sit on the edge of the bed and peer around the room. Just this morning I was thinking of this mostly as a home, and now I just think of it as my prison. How a day can change your outlook on the simplest of things.

Kathryn returns shortly with a cup of warm green tea just as she said she would. I blow on it ever so slightly and take a sip.

"Something is bothering you, Quinn." It's the first time I've heard her call me anything other than "lovely" or "dear."

I peek at her. "Yes, it is."

"Do you want to talk about it?"

If I did, what would I say? That I've betrayed all their trust? Do I throw Brett under the bus, saying it was all his idea? Do I tell her I have a child that no one knows about, including her son?

"I've lied to Brett," I say. Truth? "Well, I haven't lied, but I've kept something from him." Yes, truth.

She smooths my hair away from my face. "Is it something you feel that he needs to know?" Only a mother would ask all the right questions.

"Yes, it is."

"Then, you must tell him, dear."

I stare down into my cup. "I know. I just don't know how."

She takes the cup from my hands and sets it gently on the table. She cups my hands inside of hers. "Lies and secrets are what hurt people. Telling the truth is what keeps people together, if they're strong enough."

Are we strong enough? I'm not so sure. I've only just now come around. How do I tell a man who fell in love with a single woman that I'm actually a single mother?

"If he loves you," she begins, "and I know that he does, he will understand."

"Mom? Quinn? What's wrong? Anne said Quinn was sick?" Brett announces, bursting through the doorway and kneeling at my side.

Kathryn simply winks at me. "Everything is okay, son. Quinn just felt a little under the weather today. I'll leave you two alone." With that, she leaves us, closing the door.

21

BRETT

"WHAT'S GOING ON? Are you okay? What's wrong?"

Quinn shakes her head. "I just have a lot on my mind."

What could she have possibly shared with my mom that she can't share with me?

"You know you can tell me anything."

She peers up at me. "No, I can't."

"I don't understand."

"It's nothing. I just got a little sick today at the nail spa. Probably from the fumes."

"Well, lie down. I'll rub your back for you," I say, pulling the covers over her.

"No, Brett. Stop. I can't—" She stops herself.

"What? You can't what?"

Her eyes close, and she lowers her head. "I can't do this anymore. I need to go home."

"Why, Quinn? I don't understand. I thought things were going so well. We had a nice time the last night and with the ball game..."

"We did. I know."

I don't want her to leave. It's not about letting my family think I'm engaged anymore. Maybe I could come up with an excuse as to why she's leaving but honestly, I just don't want her to go for my own sake. I want her here with me.

I was finally starting to feel like I was making progress, making her smile. Today something happened to make that glimmer leave her eyes, and yet she won't tell me what has gone wrong or what is different.

I won't be able to take it if she leaves. Not because she is leaving me *today*, but because I know that if she leaves today, she will leave for always. I can't let that happen. I love her.

There, I said it. I love her. I would shout it from the rooftop if I thought it would make her stay with me, but knowing her, it would only make her run faster.

"Tell me what I can do to change your mind," I plead. "What has changed?"

She peeks up to meet my eyes. "Your family."

"What did they do?"

A tear falls from her eye as she shakes her head. "They loved me."

They loved her. I understand now. She loves them too, and it hurts her to lie.

I should kick myself for not imagining that would happen. I just never assumed my family would take to her so quickly or she to them. What have I done?

"Quinn, don't leave me. It doesn't matter what my family thinks anymore. I no longer want you here for their sakes. I want you here for mine. I don't want to lose you. Do you understand?"

"I have nothing to offer you," she says, stifling a cry.

"You have everything to offer me. Please."

She stares up at me and brushes her fingers through my hair

and caresses the side of my face. I close my eyes, allowing the sensation to take me over. Then I feel her breath on my lips, and I part mine slightly, finding hers.

I wipe the tears from her cheek with my thumb as I gently kiss her lips. My tongue finds hers. This is love. I can feel it.

She stops and peers at me. "Do you love me?"

I'm afraid to answer. Everything in me is screaming "yes," but each time I've tried to show her love, it's gone sour.

But I can't say no. It would be a lie to not admit my feelings for her. So, I give in.

"Yes, I do."

She closes her eyes and sinks into a fresh kiss, and I place my arms around her. This kiss doesn't feel like the other times.

It feels like the first time I've ever kissed anyone. The first time I've ever been in love with someone. The first time I've loved someone more than I love myself.

I could have loved Lisa like this, had she given me the chance, but her romance was with money. I always knew it, and I always felt it.

With Quinn, it's different. I can tell in her kiss and her touch where her heart and feelings truly lie.

We break apart. Both breathing heavily for several minutes before a word is finally spoken.

"I've never experienced anything like that before," she says.

"Because you've never been with someone who loves you as much as I do," I say, though I'm not sure if it's appropriate, but it must be true. Had Spencer felt this way for her, he would never have sought love elsewhere. I can't imagine being with anyone but her, especially after today.

It's now that I realize what she meant earlier. My family loves her. This weekend will be over soon, and what will happen after that? Do we tell them we broke up? Or now that we've admitted our love for one another—or at least I admitted my love—do we tell everyone the truth, or maybe just a version of the truth?

I'm torn between doing what's right and what's easy. What's right is for Quinn and me to come clean and admit we lied about being engaged, but we have found love in one another now and hopefully plan to be together. What's easy is just playing out the last two days like we have been and worrying about what we plan to do with our love once we arrive home. Is that truly the "easy" way? Somehow it doesn't seem like it.

————

I DECIDE I NEED ADVICE. I knock on Phil's door, and to my surprise, Fran answers.

"Fran, hey. Is Phil in here?" She opens the door fully to show Phil lying across the bed, watching the flat-screen, which is mounted on the wall above his dresser. "Can I have a few minutes alone with him?"

"Sure. I'll be downstairs, Phil," she says and promptly leaves.

He sits up in bed. "What's wrong?"

I shake my head, sucking in a long, well-deserved breath. "I'm not sure. Nothing is wrong, I suppose. I'm just trying to decide if everything is *right* now."

"What do you mean?" he asks, patting the bed for me to take a seat. I opt to sit in the tall, wingback chair in the corner, still wiping sweat from around my neck.

"It's Quinn. I think she loves me," I say, still having trouble believing it myself.

His eyes widen. "She does? Well, you feel the same, right?"

I nod. "Yeah, I do. I'm just not sure what to do with the information now that I have it."

"What do you mean?"

I tilt my head. "I don't feel right about lying to my family anymore."

"There are only two more days, and then you go home."

"I know, but what led up to Quinn telling me she loved me was her not wanting to lie to them anymore either. She said she knows my family loves her, and I think she loves them, too."

"Where is Quinn now?"

"Asleep. I, uh, admitted my love for her over some steamy kissing."

"That good, huh?"

I blush a bit but shake it off. "It's not like that, Phil. We shared a moment. I've got to tell you, I've never experienced love like this before, as cliché as that sounds."

"No, I... I know what you mean," he says.

I cock my head. "You mean you and..."

"Yeah, me and Fran."

I chuckle. "Well, did I interrupt just now?"

He laughs. "No, it's like you said, it's not like that. It's not about just sex for us. We're in love."

"You're sure she feels the same way, too?"

"Yeah, I'm sure."

I take his offer to sit next to him on the bed now, and I clap his shoulder. "I've never known you to be in love before, or at least not admit to it."

"Because it's never happened to me before. I guess I never took women seriously until I met her. I always wanted someone to love, but I was afraid to put myself out there. Her refusal lit a fire in me when I met her. With all the time we've spent alone since being here, I suppose it was bound to happen. I love her. I can see myself building a life with her someday."

"That's amazing, man! I'm happy for you."

"So, what are you going to do now?" he asks, eying me.

I shake my head and shrug. "I don't know. I guess only time will tell. When she wakes up, I'll ask her what she wants to do, and we'll do it."

"If she decides she wants to tell your folks the truth, what do you think will happen?"

"I think they'll look at her differently—look at us both differently, I assume—but I've already done so many things wrong in this relationship that I have to do what's right now. There's just no way around it anymore."

Everything I'm saying I know is true, but I also know everything is easier said than done. I don't want my family to look at Quinn as someone who conned them. It doesn't matter how they look at me because we are family and will always get past our troubles, but I want to start a life with Quinn. I have to find a way to make them understand.

Make them understand that it was me who did this and not her. I want to make sure they know she didn't want to originally, but I forced her hand. Although, I can't tell them why she agreed to do it. Some things, even if they are the truth, are better left unsaid.

I return to our room where Quinn is still sleeping, having never moved. Her hair is awry, hanging down in her face and upon her shoulders. The warm glow of the sunset from the window reflects off her skin.

For the first time in a long time, I'm thankful. I'm thankful that this doesn't scare Quinn away like many other attempts at love have. I'm thankful I have made her forget about Spencer and others that have hurt her. Lastly, I'm thankful that she focuses now on what could be and knows that when I said I love her, it was the truth.

I sit on the edge of the bed and smooth the hair from her face, and she stirs only a moment in her sleep. She must be dreaming something beautiful because for the first time since we've been here, I see her smiling as she dreams. I hope she awakes with a newfound look on life and that she finds comfort in what has come to be between us. I hope.

22

QUINN

I AWAKEN but am afraid to move. What have I done? It will never be okay to love him. He doesn't know anything about the real me. At least that's what I'm telling myself now.

So he knows I like sports and found being wined and dined exhilarating. That could be any number of women. He doesn't know about the most important person in my life: my daughter.

When he finds out that I have kept her from him, what will happen? Will he be shocked? Of course. Will he be angry? I imagine so.

If I leave now, say my goodbyes, and make my apologies to the family, I can leave in peace and never see Brett again. I can leave him with a good memory of me. I can leave him knowing that I do care for him and I showed it, but I have to leave. There's no way around it.

I turn my head slightly and see he is asleep in the chair next to the bed. It's dark out, and I glance to my other side at the clock to see it's just past nine.

"You're awake," he says, and I'm startled.

I can feel my heart begin beating faster, and my breathing becomes heavy. I don't even know where to begin. This should have never happened. He sits on the edge of the bed next to me and runs his fingers through my hair, but I finagle away from his hand.

"What's wrong?"

"I have to leave, Brett."

"What? I thought we were past that. What about…"

"That should have never happened. I'm sorry."

"What are you talking about? You're the one who initiated that. You're the one who asked if I loved you, and the answer is yes, I do."

I shake my head, trying to erase his entire sentence from my head. "No, I can't stay here."

"Tell me why!" he exclaims.

"Because there's things about me you don't know!" I holler back.

He grabs my arms and holds me steady as I stand, his voice now barely above a whisper. "Don't do this, Quinn. Don't run away."

"I'm not running away. I just… You don't know everything about me."

"So, what? You don't know everything about me either. If there's something I need to know, then tell me, but don't run away. Don't leave like this."

I shrug his hands off me and grab my empty suitcase.

"So, that's it then? You're going to leave in the middle of the night as if you're trying to escape from some prison, and for what? So, you can go back to *him*?"

I turn to face him. What does he know?

"Yeah, Quinn. I know all about Spencer wanting you back. I just can't believe that the person I've grown to know and love would even give him a second glance."

I turn back around and throw random clothes into my bag.

"You don't know what you're talking about," I say, though apparently, he does. I'm going to kill Fran.

"Quinn, you can't do this. What is your reason for leaving me in the dead of night to go to him?" He grabs me and turns me to face him. Practically nose to nose, he stares into my eyes, "Tell me the truth."

I yank until his hands release me. "I never said I was going back to Spencer."

"No, you didn't say it, but you are, aren't you? I know you better than you know yourself, Quinn. I knew the moment I admitted that I loved you that it would scare the crap out of you—the minute you realized that this was more than just an agreement.

"But I took the chance. I told you I love you. I've loved you from day one. I won't let you go without a fight."

"We said no strings attached," I remind him.

"Forget strings. You're not worried about strings. For some reason, you can't let him go, and you can't recognize true love when it's staring you in the face. It's right here, Quinn. I'm standing right here. Love. You're running away from it."

I turn around to him and open my mouth, but no words come. I stand there like a fool who is transparent, and everyone can see right through me.

"I felt you, Quinn. I've touched you. Tell me I haven't touched your heart, and I'll let you leave. I'll even drive you to the airport myself, but only if you can look at me and tell me you don't love me."

I bite my cheek, and my eyes fill with tears. I want to tell him the truth. I want everything to be okay, but that will never happen. He loves a woman who doesn't exist. So once again, as I have this entire trip, I lie.

"I don't love you."

His eyes close, and I can almost hear his heart breaking. I

feel a rumble in my own that I only recognize as agony. I zip my bag and leave, heading for Fran's room.

I open the door without knocking and find her in bed, reading. "Get packed if you're going with me. I'm leaving."

"You're leaving? What are you talking about?"

"I just can't do this anymore. Get packed. I'm not staying here another night."

I leave the room and walk downstairs to gather more of my belongings. There, sitting on the edge of the sofa, is the softball glove he bought me. I pick it up, twisting it in my hands. The ring on my finger—the one that started it all—glitters in the moonlight leaking in through the long, glass windows. I set the glove down, go to the window, and finally allow myself to cry.

"Quinn?" A voice I've grown to love asks.

I sniffle and stifle further tears from falling, wiping away the few strays with the back of my hand. "Yes ma'am," I answer Kathryn.

"What's wrong, dear?" She puts her arms around me, and everything that I have been holding in for days pours out of me as if someone turned on a faucet. To hug a mother again is what I've needed. She would have made for a perfect one, had I listened to Fran in the first place and given Brett a real chance.

All that is past now. I'm in too deep to pull a child from my hat like a magic trick. All is lost. I know that now.

"I have to go home," I tell her.

She stares into my eyes as if she knows the real truth and wipes a tear from my eye with her handkerchief. "You mean you *want* to go home," she counters.

I lower my head. "I couldn't bring myself to tell him."

"Would it help if you told me?"

I consider her offer. It would be nice to sit and talk to my mother again, but I will never have that option. Here is a mother, asking me what's wrong, wanting to talk to me, and all I want to do in this world right now is say, yes. So, for the first time since I've been here, I tell the truth.

"Yes, ma'am. It would help. Though, I'm afraid you will look at me differently. I'm not who I seem."

She shakes her head and makes a clicking sound with her tongue between her teeth. "You think we all don't know that?"

My head jerks up, and I meet her eyes. "You mean..."

"Oh, we don't know the whole story, I'm sure, but we know there's more to your and Brett's relationship than meets the eye."

"So much more," I mumble.

"Here," she says, taking me by the arm. "I'll make us a spot of tea and we'll talk."

I smile through my tears and, in that moment, realize that's exactly what I need. I need a mother, I need the tea, and most importantly, I need to talk.

I need to air everything out, at least to one person who is unbiased. Well, partly. I know her main concern will be for her son, but if I'm correct, she has grown to love me and will understand the predicament I now find myself in.

"Tell me what ails you," she says, pouring tea from a silver kettle.

"I've lied, well, *we've* lied to everyone. What's worse, I lied to Brett, or rather kept the truth from him."

"What is the truth?"

I swallow hard. "I have a daughter."

She tilts her head in question. "How have you managed to keep that from Brett when you two are engaged?"

"That's just it. We aren't engaged, Kathryn. I needed, or at least thought I needed, a favor from Brett. So, he agreed to help in exchange for my posing as his fiancé this week. He didn't do it to hurt any of you. On the contrary, he just wanted to make you happy."

She puts her hand to her face. "Oh dear, I suppose I have been putting a lot of pressure on him to find someone, but it's only because I didn't want him to be alone. He's such a good boy. He deserves to be happy like his father and I are. That's all I wanted for him."

"I think he knows that," I say, "but a child will do almost anything to please a parent. I know I would if I had the chance again."

"You mean..."

"Yes, ma'am," I answer. "I lost my mother some time ago."

"Your father?"

"Has a new family elsewhere."

"Oh, my poor dear," she says, placing her hand upon mine, "I'm so sorry to hear that."

"The truth is, I love your family, and I just can't lie to you any longer, and I can't tell Brett about my daughter."

"Why not? Brett will understand."

I shake my head. "I'm not so sure. He admitted he's in love with me today, but how much will he love me when he finds out I'm not alone in this world like he thinks? I have a child to think about. I never told him about her because she just witnessed her father and I divorcing, and I didn't want her to get attached to another man who might end up leaving her. I can't ask Brett to just be okay with something like this either. He doesn't love me. He loves who I've pretended to be these past couple weeks."

"I don't think you give Brett enough credit, Quinn. If he says he loves you, then he does, and you can't fall out of love with someone so quickly. When you love someone, you accept their faults, their interests, their loves, and in your case, he would accept your daughter. Brett loves children. You've seen him with Nell," she says.

I nod. "I know. Maybe I'm the one who can't face the truth.

Now my ex-husband wants to reconcile, and I feel like I should give him another chance for our daughter's sake."

"Do you love your ex-husband?"

"Yes, I do."

"Do you love Brett?" she asks.

I nod. "Yes."

She pats my hand. "Then go home, sweetie. You need time to yourself to figure out what is best for you and your daughter."

"But Brett— "

"I'll look after Brett, dear. Don't you worry," she assures me.

I kiss her on the cheek and hug her just as Fran is coming down the stairs with her bag and the taxi cab arrives. "I'm sorry to leave so suddenly."

"You have to do what's best for you." She gives me one last kiss, and I'm out the door, away from this family and away from Brett.

I hate myself for the way I left him. The last thing I said to him was I didn't love him. Lie. He wouldn't have let me leave any other way, though, and I want to see where things go with Spencer.

I have to give my marriage one last chance for Evie's sake. She would love for her dad and me to reconcile, and now that Melissa is out of the picture, we have a real chance. Fran seems to think that if he cheated once, he will again, but that would be admitting that people can't change, and I'm a firm believer in the fact that people can. I have to ride this horse until the end.

Suddenly, I miss Evie too much to stay another minute. I can't wait to see her smiling face and smell the sweet scent of her shampoo as she hugs me. Oh, how I miss that smell.

"I'm sorry," I tell Fran.

"Don't be sorry. I can tell when you're at your breaking point. I just don't understand why."

"I'll explain it all to you. I promise."

"It's going to be hard to get a direct flight back to New York City this late at night," she reminds me.

"Honestly, that's the least of my worries."

So here we are, on our way back home. The moonlight shines above us and reflects off the windows of the cab. I trace the reflection with my finger. I've never doubted whether I was doing the right or the wrong thing as much as I have the past two weeks. For now, the right thing to do is to go home and plan on doing what's best for Evie.

23

BRETT

"WHAT DO YOU MEAN SHE LEFT?" asks Anne, as I try to come up with a reasonable explanation of why Quinn has taken off.

"She had a family emergency she had to get to."

"You didn't go with her?" asks Russ. "That's not like you."

"Son, that's not how I raised you at all," my father chimes in, nostrils flared.

"Father..."

"I'm sure there's a rational explanation for why he's not going, and it's not any of our business. It's theirs," says my mother. Everyone suddenly stares at her. It's not like my mother to let something like this go so easily.

"Well, I hate that she's gone," Anne says. "I hope everything is okay."

"Me, too. I miss her," says Nell. I pick Nell up and twirl her around.

"Well, you still have me here," I tell her. She giggles, but it fades away quickly.

"I wanted to play softball again," she says. "Aunt Quinn let me be umpire."

I set her down and rub the top of her head, messing up her freshly combed hair. "It's okay, sport."

"Do you know what the family emergency was?" asks Russ.

I shake my head. "Not entirely sure. She told me to stay here and not to worry. She took Fran with her, though. She'll be okay."

I'm not sure how convincing I am or why my mother jumped to my side so quickly, but I'm also not sure what else I can say to make them believe me. My world is upside down, and I feel nauseated. She never told me she loved me, though I thought it was implied when she asked if I loved her. Hearing her say the words "I don't love you" was heartbreaking, to say the least.

Heartbreaking is not even the correct word. Somehow, for the first time in my life, any word I think of seems to fall short of how I truly feel. What has this woman done to me? And what secrets did she keep from me?

———

PHIL MEETS me a bit later in my room. I'm sure I'm an awful sight: shirt untucked, hair sticking up, and sitting on the edge of my bed in shambles. I don't even glance up to see who has entered. I already know by the heavy footsteps that almost skipped up the stairs happily.

"What's the real story, bro?" he asks as he sits, leaning forward to mock my posture.

"I'm not even sure where to start," I say, shaking my head, still in disbelief. "I can promise you, though, she's probably on her way to crawl back to her ex."

"No, not Quinn. She's too tough for a move like that."

"Oh, she's tough all right, but her head is so messed up that she has mine done in, too."

"Tell me what happened."

"I think we love each other."

"So? What else is new?" he laughs.

"No. I mean she implied that she loved me and I her. Everything was perfect."

"I remember you saying that, but what went wrong then?"

I shake my head, and my eyes dart around the room, searching for an answer. "I guess it scared her."

"Scared her?"

"Yeah. She's scared to be in love with me for some reason. I guess it means she'd have to let go of her ex, and I just don't think she's ready to do that. I just don't know why he has this hold on her."

"What did he put her through?"

"He cheated. Some stripper he met. He left her high and dry. Now he wants her back, and I suppose she wants to see where it goes."

"So, you're giving up this easy? You said you loved her. Fight for her," he says. "You're the better man. We all know that."

"I shouldn't have to!" I almost holler. "Love isn't supposed to be hard. It's supposed to be natural."

"Who said love isn't hard? Just because it's not hard for one person doesn't mean it's easy for us all. If you let her go, that's on you, not her. It's time to man up." He claps me on the shoulder and leaves, and I'm left wondering if he's right or if I am.

Love certainly wasn't easy for Lisa and me, but I know that wasn't my fault. I had no alternative but to give up on her. She never loved me. But Quinn does. I know from the way she showed me with her words and her kisses.

"Honey?" my mother's voice sounds from the door.

"Yeah, Mom. Come in."

She sits on the edge of the bed Phil vacated. "I'm sorry."

"For what?"

"This is all my fault, dear." I glance to her, thinking that it probably is, but I let that moment melt from my mind. It's all my fault, no one else's. "I put too much pressure on you to find someone."

I pat her hand. "No, Mom. You didn't. This isn't anyone's fault. She had a family emergency. It couldn't be helped."

"Brett, let's agree not to lie to one another anymore," she says, and I wince.

"Lie?"

"Quinn talked me to last night before she left."

"What did Quinn say?" I already know, but I'm surprised she chose my mother to confide in. Maybe she had to tell someone, and who better to understand than a mother?

"She said you didn't want to come alone and that she agreed to pretend you were a couple. Honey, you shouldn't have made her or anyone pretend. That young lady shouldn't have been put through all this just for my sake."

My head slumps, and I feel deflated. "It wasn't for your sake." She eyes me. "Okay, it wasn't *just* for your sake, but it's over now. She's on her way home to be with the man she truly loves."

"Oh, honey, Quinn loves you. There are just things you don't know."

"Why does everyone keep saying that?" I ask angrily. "*What* don't I know?"

"It's not my place to tell you, but I can tell you this—Quinn loves you. She told me she did, and I could see in her eyes that it was true. She's just confused and needs time to sort things out. Surely you can understand that."

"Mom, I just want to be with her. I don't want to go back

home and see her walking the streets of Manhattan with that jerk-off she was married to before."

"I know, I know, but this is Quinn's life. You put her in this position. These are the consequences. You have to give her time, and if you love her, then her feelings should come before your own."

I know she is right. I've heard that my whole life, but when you are in the thick of it all, you feel quite differently. All I can concentrate on at the moment is what I can do to make my own pain go away.

I go back and forth for the next several hours about whether my mother is right or if Phil is right. Do I go catch a flight and run after her, fight for her as Phil suggested? Or do I spend my last day on the beach while she works out what she wants, which might be her first husband, if I'm taken out of the equation.

I need different points of view. I can't go at this alone. I think it's time I come clean with the rest of my family.

24

QUINN

"QUINN! JUST TALK TO ME!" Fran shrills in my ear, but I ignore her. This cab ride is taking forever. I just want to get to the airport, board the plane, go home, and forget I was ever even here.

What have I done? I scream inside my head. I rub my temples and want to cry, but no tears come. What was I thinking, implying to Brett that I loved him? As if this trip wasn't the dumbest thing I had ever done, I had to add insult to injury. Story of my life.

I do love him, but it was stupid of me to ask him that when I know I love Spencer, too. Especially when I knew I'd give Spencer another chance for Evie's sake. Maybe for my own sake, too. I'm a creature of habit, if nothing else. I feel comfortable with Spencer. He's all I've ever known.

Yes, he made a mistake, but we all do, don't we? It could have just as easily been me that messed up, and looking at things now, that's a distinct possibility. Spencer wants to come home.

Now I see Brett's face in my head. I close my eyes and try to shake the vision away, but there he is at the jewelry shop. I glance down at my ring, and there he is on the beach and on our makeshift softball field. I crack a smile, thinking of when he told me he's always loved me.

There he is again at the zoo, showing me my favorite animal in the world, giraffes, and again on the tram, hanging thousands of feet in the air by only wires, and again toasting to our newfound friendship, and once more, showing me the real way to eat seafood. He taught me so much during this trip about myself and life.

I still don't understand how he could have always loved me. He doesn't know the true me. The broken me. The me with a child to raise. He'll never understand.

Spencer does though. Spencer knows I'm broken, and we share a child together, which Brett would never understand. For all I know, Brett doesn't even like children. Well, he loves Nell, but what does that prove?

We board the plane, and I feel less comfortable than I thought I would. In all honesty, I'm freaking out more now than I ever have. Fran has finally given up yelling at me for answers, but I grab her hand and squeeze it. She stares at me.

"Fran, I'm so scared."

"Just tell me what this is all about."

I duck my head. "I, uh, told Brett that I loved him. Well, in not so many words. It scares the crap out of me."

"So, you're scared of loving Brett?"

"I think at this point I'm scared of everything."

"Do you?"

"Do I what?"

"Do you love him?"

I nod almost frantically. "I do, but I love Spencer, too."

She tilts her head in what I can only assume is pity. "You're leaving Brett for Spencer? Oh, honey."

"I have to try, Fran. For Evie's sake."

"Going back to Spencer won't make Evie happy, Quinn. She's getting more attention from her father now than she ever has. If you go back to Spencer, you won't find peace. Evie won't have this great family life you think she will have. You will both be miserable, and it would only be a matter of time before things fall apart again."

"What do you mean by that?"

"Do you truly think Spencer has had some sort of epiphany since he's been gone? I can promise you anything that Melissa left him, and that's the only reason he wants you back. He can't be alone. Much like you." She mumbles the last sentence under her breath, but I hear it loud and clear."

She takes my hands in hers. "Quinn, I love you more than I love anyone on this planet. You're my best friend and my only family. Tell me, what are you afraid of at this moment? Not what you're afraid of in the future or what you're afraid of once you get home. What are you afraid of *right now*?"

My brows push together for a moment in thought. My hands grip hers tightly. "This plane leaving."

She shakes her head. "Then why are we on it?"

Tears stream down my face. "We're not. Let's go."

As the last passengers are streaming in through the door, Fran and I grab our bags and run for the exit, squeezing our way past them as the stewardess yells our way. Once we're back inside the airport, we try to call Phil's phone, but we can't seem to get a signal.

We flag down a cab letting out another person near the curb close to the door. We give him the beach house address, and once again we are back on our way to paradise. Although, if I'm being honest, Malibu doesn't hold any allure for me any longer.

What am I doing now? The right thing? I *think* so. If what Fran says is true, then this is the path I should take. It scares me, but when did I decide that giving Spencer a second chance was the best thing for me?

Kathryn told me to go home. She told me to go home and work out my problems. Should I have done that? Or maybe, just maybe, I already have.

25

BRETT

I CAN SEE what I've done wrong now. Nothing is Quinn's fault. I pushed her. I begged her. Maybe I even manipulated her without realizing it.

She wasn't ready for all of this. I was plucked from a crowd when she seduced me with her words. I, in turn, forced her hand. Had I just stuck to the original rules, we both would have had a fun time and split ways long ago. Not because it would have never worked between us—it could have—but because I wouldn't have been trying to win her over. I did manipulate her.

She would be with her ex-husband right now, not giving me a second thought, but I ruined that for her. Oh, she may go back to her ex-husband, but there's a weight on her shoulders now. One I can take off her now that I know it's my own fault and misfortune.

Janine was right, and I'm kicking myself for thinking I was above her maturity level. She knew something none of the rest of us did. She knew someone would get hurt. I'm hurt, and I believe Quinn is, too.

It hurt to be told she didn't love me. I can't deny that. I don't believe it's true, though. I believe she loves me but only because I basically tricked her into loving me with fancy dinners and playing on her passions and emotions, and played on her vulnerability. Not that I recognized it then, but I do now.

I showered her with love and giraffes, wine and jewelry. What a schemer I was. I scold myself now, staring into the mirror that I'd like to punch.

I sent Phil to round up my family. Even my niece thought she was gaining an aunt, friend, and playmate. Then, I ripped that away from her.

Even worse, I dangled Quinn in front of my family like a trophy I had won, when in reality, I'm just a fraud in love. I'm selfish and conniving, and though I tried to take Quinn's feelings into account, I was only worried about my own the whole time.

Maybe I thought I could blind her with how wonderful I could make life for her, but I know little of her life before me. Perhaps it was better. Maybe her ex-husband did make a mistake that he is sincerely sorry for and they can once again build a life together.

The fight in me is gone. All that remains is the broken man I started out as before I met her. For now, I need to confess my manipulation to my family and accept whatever looks, thoughts, or words they give me once the air is clear.

"Everyone's here," Phil says, as I trudge my way down the stairs and into the main room.

My mother and father sit on the couch with Russ. Anne sits upon the arm of the sofa, and little Nell stands in front of her, fidgeting with her dress.

When my feet hit the wooden floor, I finally peer up to meet their wondering faces. My mother gives me a nod. Maybe by coming clean, I'm making her proud of me.

It feels good to think that. I hadn't considered that she

177

would be proud of me for being honest before now. Between Phil and Mom, I have some allies here. I'm not standing alone.

"What's going on, Brett?" Anne asks, gripping her daughter's shoulders.

I place my hands in my pockets and lower my head for only a moment, sucking in a deep breath before staring at them once more. "I've lied to you all. I've deceived you."

"What are you talking about?"

I lick my lips. "Quinn isn't my fiancé. We aren't even dating. I lied to you. Phil and Fran, they lied for us."

"Then who is she, son?" my father asks, leaning in closer.

How do I explain to them who she is?

"The truth is I don't even know her that well. Well, I didn't when I invited her here. I knew if I came alone..." I stop myself. Don't use excuses, Brett. You've done enough to your family. Man up. "The truth is, she's the woman I love, but she didn't leave here because of a family emergency. She left here because she wants to give her ex-husband another chance, and I'm choosing not to stand in her way. I'm sorry that I lied to you, to all of you. It wasn't my intention to hurt anyone."

"So, Quinn isn't going to be my aunt?" Nell asks.

I swallow hard and glance to Anne who shakes her head at me.

"I don't think so, kiddo."

"Son," my father says. "You love this woman?"

I nod. "Yeah, Pop. I do."

I see Anne crack a smile, staring past me. "Then here's your chance."

"Brett?" I hear a voice say. I turn quickly to peer behind me, and there stands the woman I love.

"Quinn?" She nods. "I thought you were on a plane."

"Change of plans."

I smile widely, but quickly I'm reminded of my manipulation, and my smile turns downward.

"Excuse me, guys," I tell my family, grabbing Quinn by the arm as Fran walks past us to hug Phil. I take her outside where the others can't hear and shut the door behind us.

"What are you doing here?"

She shakes her head and shrugs. "I just finally know what I want."

"How?"

"Fran asked me what I was most afraid of."

"And?"

"I said leaving."

"Why?" I ask.

"Because it meant leaving you behind."

I want to smile. I want to, but I don't. I know that she needs to do what she set out to do or she will always wonder if she and her ex could have worked it out.

"Go home, Quinn."

She was only just reaching out to hold me, but now her hands fall to her sides before folding across her chest. "What?"

I unfold her arms, taking her hands in mine. "Go home. I love you. I love you so much that I can't manipulate you anymore. I pushed you too hard. So hard that you were running away to be with another man. You say there's things I don't know. Things you are afraid to tell me."

"But I'm not afraid anymore. I came here to—"

"No, Quinn. I want you to be happy. You'll never be happy with me. All this," I say, waving my arms about, "it's tainted. We can't come back from this."

"We can, though."

I shake my head and drop my hands. "Quinn, you're not in love with me. You may think you are now, but you're not. Maybe I'm not either."

I see the words cut through her like a knife, but what choice did I have? Even if she *was* serious today, tomorrow she would just change her mind again. She's done it time and time again. Until this Spencer thing is past her, she's no good to anyone... not even herself.

I have to sit here and watch her ride off with Fran in a cab once more. It doesn't hurt as much this time because I finally feel like I'm thinking of her rather than myself. I do love her. That alone proves it to me. My family, on the other hand, is not so understanding.

"What is going on?" Anne asks, and I wince at her words. The rest of the family has scattered, but I should have seen this bullet coming a mile away.

"I'm sorry, Anne. What can I say?"

"Why are you apologizing to *me*?"

"Who else would I apologize to?"

"Quinn!" she hollers, pointing in the direction the cab left.

"I gave Quinn what she needed."

"She needed to be turned down by the man she loves?" she asks, quite upset.

"Anne! Just stop. You don't understand anything about this. I'm sorry I lied to you all, but you don't know what that woman and I have been through—what she's put me through or what I've put her through."

"You're right. I don't, but I know that despite what you've put one another through, she came back, with her tail between her legs, wanting *you*."

"Quinn doesn't know what she wants."

"Son," I hear my mother say, much more calmly than Anne. "A woman always knows what she wants. Sometimes it's just hard to admit to it."

"Then how do I know she's just not admitting to herself that she wants Spencer?"

She shakes her head. "You don't, but when you love her and she loves you, you have to give the relationship a chance. You can't be jury, judge, and executioner of this girl.

"She came here ready to reveal all to you, and let me tell you, that doesn't come easy. You sent her away without so much as hearing her out."

"Dad, back me up here," I beg of him.

"Son, I told you before that I knew your relationship with this girl wasn't all you said it was, but seeing her come all the way back here just to profess her love makes me believe that it could be. Your sister and mother are right. People will always tell you to remember the happy times. I won't say that. I say remember the tough times, because the tough times are what get you from one happy time to the next. Go after her, son."

I rub my eyelids, tired, confused, and worn out. I head to my room where I can actually think for myself, and I place a hand up to stop Phil from following me. I close the door to the room and lie on the bed. On the nightstand is my old note to her and a wilted flower.

My phone rings, but I don't recognize the number.

"Hello?"

"Are you crazy or something?"

"Fran?"

"Do you know what that girl went through to get back to you?"

I close my eyes. "Fran, it was for her own good. I didn't do it for me. I did it for her."

"We'll you're going to have to do a lot of convincing to get me to believe that one."

"She loves Spencer," I remind her.

"Yeah. So? She has her reasons for thinking she loves Spencer, but she's *in* love with *you*."

"What reasons?"

"I'm not going to tell you. She was trying to tell you, and you blew her off. She came back to explain everything, and you broke her."

"She was already broken."

"Brett, she wasn't asking you for a marriage proposal. She wasn't asking you for anything you didn't already promise to give her. You told her you wouldn't be something she had to survive, yet here she is, trying to survive you."

I did tell her that. I did. I close my eyes and feel tears finally swell up. "Fran, I love her so much that it hurts. I thought I was doing what was best."

"You know what kind of man Spencer is. I told you, and she told you. Do you think driving her into his arms is what's best for her?"

"I don't know anymore."

"Well, if I were you, I'd figure it out quick. Because you may have just driven the woman you love into the arms of another man... for good."

26

QUINN

HE THINKS HE MANIPULATED ME. He didn't. I've manipulated everyone from day one. Even worse, I've pushed everyone away. Fran won't admit it and would never leave my side, but I know she didn't want to leave Phil behind.

I've turned Brett's world upside down and made my own practically unlivable. I know he'll never forgive me. All I can do now is try to move forward and forget about him. Forget the candlelit dinners and the way he went out of his way to make me feel so welcome and comfortable. I can't let myself feel those things again.

I'm like a hurricane, destroying everything in my path. I destroy lives. At least one good thing came from all of this—Fran has finally found happiness.

"So, when are you supposed to see each other again?" I ask her, trying to keep my mind far away from Brett *and* Spencer.

"When he gets back." Her answers are short and obvious. I'm not sure if it's because she would rather not talk to me or because she is trying to spare me from small talk, but as we enter my house, I finally feel the lump in my throat.

I have missed home. I miss the days when things made sense. I can honestly say, even after Spencer cheated and I left, that things still seemed normal. Cheating happens every day, and I was determined to not go through life as a victim.

I had Evie to keep me grounded and on the straight and narrow, or so I thought before my drunken fall from reality two weeks ago. I escape to the bathroom to freshen up from our plane ride. The mirror mocks me. It shows me a beautiful woman who seems like she could have anything in the world. Lies.

I twist the heart-shaped ring on my finger and glare down at it, disgusted. My mother would be ashamed of me. I take the ring off, placing it in the soap dish nearby. I run the water over my hands and splash some onto my face. I don't bother to pat it dry.

I walk backwards from the sink and find the door, sliding down it and landing on the floor. My breaking point. Tears fall freely from my eyes and mix with the water. I wipe my nose with the back of my hand and tuck my hair behind my ears. What have I done?

Knock. Knock. "Quinn?"

"Yeah, I'll be out in a minute," I answer.

"Quinn, let me in or come out."

I close my eyes tight. I know she won't go away until I do what she wants. Still, I sit in silence for another minute or two, staring at a cracked tile in the floor until I hear her yet again.

Knock. Knock. "I'm not going away."

I laugh sarcastically through my nose. I find the will to stand once more and open the door to her concerned face.

"Quinn," she sighs.

"I'm okay. Just needed a minute."

"Come lie down with me. It's been a long day." We lie on the bed facing each other, and again the tears start falling.

184

"What have I done?" I ask her.

She shakes her head. "Made a mess, but it's nothing that can't be fixed with time."

"I don't know what I'm doing anymore."

"I don't know what you were doing to start with," she laughs.

I laugh at my own disaster. "I don't know. I guess I was trying to show myself that I can be in control of my own life."

"That's a woman's greatest lie. Every woman thinks she is in control of her life until that one man shows up. Then they see how unraveled they truly are. I think Brett did you a service."

I squint. "What do you mean?"

"He opened you back up. You were able to look past the meaningless sex you wanted and actually love someone again. You ended up offering yourself to a guy who cared for you, or learned to. You're lucky. Imagine how you'd be feeling if he just used you and then left."

My lips purse. "I thought I wouldn't care."

"Yeah, but you would have. You're not a prostitute, Quinn. You're not cheap either. You're a classy lady, and don't you go forgetting that."

Knock. Knock. I roll my eyes as the sound of someone knocking on my front door echoes all the way to the bedroom where we lie.

"Who is that?" she asks.

"Can only be one person." I push myself off the bed and walk through the living room. I'm not in the mood for this.

"Thomas," I say as I open the door. "How'd you know I was home?"

"I was at the neighbor's house. I saw the taxi drop you and Fran off."

"Look, Thomas, I'm not in the mood for—"

He puts up a hand. "I'm just here as your friend, Quinn." I

stare at him. I'm not in the position to turn down a friend. "You look awful."

"I feel awful."

"Was the week that rough?" he asks.

"It depends. Does it make you happy?"

His brows push together. "Quinn, it's still me. My loving you means that if you're unhappy, then I'm unhappy. I can't believe you'd ask me that."

I exhale a deep breath. "I'm sorry, Thomas. Yeah, it was a rough week, and it didn't end well."

"I figured as much, since you're home a day early."

"Thomas," Fran says, now exiting the bedroom.

"Hey, Fran. I can see how Quinn's time went, but did you have a good time?"

"It wasn't too shabby," she says, now heading for the kitchen.

"She fell in love," I tell him.

"Now did I use the word love?" she asks. "I don't think so. I just..." She searches for the right words.

"Fell in love," Thomas and I say together. We chuckle. She brings in three glasses and a bottle of cheap red wine, pouring them to the rims for all of us.

"It's been a long week for us all. Let's toast to this catastrophe," she says.

Our glasses chime, and I love the familiar feeling of just being the three of us again. I take a larger than average gulp of wine and clap my hands together. "Who wants to paint?"

We dig through the bag with the paintbrushes and rollers and open the red, black, blue, and white paint we've been using on Evie's walls to paint white clouds and lady bugs on a sky-blue wall. I called Spencer on the way home and told him to bring Evie because I was back early. He seemed all too eager, and wouldn't you know it, twenty minutes into our little painting session, he shows up.

"Thanks for bringing her," I tell him as Evie hugs my waist before sprinting to her room to see Fran and Thomas.

"I always thought you looked best like this," he says.

"Like this?"

"Yeah. Hair tied up, over-sized shirt, baggy pants, barefoot, no makeup."

I want to smile, but I can't. Not even a fake one. I have nothing to offer.

I used to be able to read people right away. I would know how they were feeling or if they were truthful or not, but I'm wiped out. I'm not sure if I can't decide anymore, or if I'm just too tired to try.

"I have to get back to painting. Fran and Thomas are here helping me."

"Can I come by tomorrow, Quinn? I'd like to talk to you."

My heart races, and my breathing halts. I can only muster enough strength to barely nod.

"I'll see you then."

I shut the door and lean against it. I already know what he wants. He wants me to come back. I just don't know why. Did he leave Melissa for me, or did she leave him?

When I enter Evie's room, a playful paint fight has ensued, and I laugh, thankful for the plastic on the floor.

"All right. All right. Break it up. Evie, come with me," I say.

Her ponytail swings back and forth and she skips to me, dropping her paintbrush on the plastic as she leaves.

"Go wait for Momma in my bedroom, okay?"

"Okay."

Fran sees the expression on my face. "What is it?"

I shake my head. "This time I'm not jumping to any conclusions. I'm going to ask Evie what *she* wants."

"Quinn," Thomas says. "You're going to base your whole life on what an eight-year-old wants?" I don't answer.

I close the door to my room, and Evie sits perfectly with her dress fanned out on the middle of my bed. I stifle a tear, sniffing and leaning my head back to stop it.

"Momma, what's wrong?"

"Nothing's wrong, baby. Why?"

"You look sad."

I wipe my hand over my mouth and sit on the bed beside her. "Are you happy here with Momma?"

She nods. Her long brown hair and cat green eyes mirror my own, and it's as though a young me answers the questions for the adult me.

"What about Daddy? Are you happy when you go to Daddy's house?"

"Yes, I'm happy at Daddy's house. I don't like the fighting, but Melissa doesn't live with Daddy anymore."

"What about when Daddy and Momma were together? Were you happy then?"

"I was always happy with you and Daddy."

I gulp. This is the first hard conversation I've ever had with my daughter. I try to keep her out of adult affairs, and I always acted happy around Evie. She didn't know how unhappy I was or apparently how unhappy her father was.

"Why, Momma?"

I wipe the stray hairs from her face and tuck them behind her ears. "You ready to paint some more?"

"Yes!" she says, clapping her hands and jumping off the bed, sprinting from the room.

She says she's happy either way now that Melissa is gone. Am I happy away from Spencer? Do I wait for Brett to get home and try to talk to him again?

I suppose Thomas was right. I can't leave this in the hands of my eight-year-old. Although, I suppose I would have had her answers been different, but now I have to do what's best for me.

27

BRETT

I WAS WORRIED about my family looking at me differently because I lied to them. On the contrary, they look at me differently for sending Quinn away. I could say I had no choice, but it would be chasing a lie. I could have told her to stay, be with me, live happily ever after, but she would always wonder what it would have been like with Spencer. I can't have that hanging over my head.

I would constantly be in fear. Ever since I started with this girl, I've been in fear. I walk on eggshells for everything I do or say. That's no way to live, and honestly, her living with doubt is no way to either.

I did it for the both of us, but that's not how my family sees it, as they sit here during my love intervention.

"Anne, I told you, even if I wanted her back, I couldn't ask her. I sent her away."

"Son, she will forgive you. She loves you," my mother coos.

I drop my head in my hands in frustration.

She will never forgive me. I know her too well. I scared her when I was simply trying to woo her. How could she forgive me after she came here to profess her love and I sent her away without even hearing her out?

Why didn't I at least hear her out? The more my family talks, the more I want to slap myself.

"She will forgive you, if you give her a reason," Russ assures me.

"What reason would I give her?" A question no one can answer. "What I did was justified. She loves another man."

"Son, she loves you. She was certain when she returned. She had made her decision," my father says.

"Dad, she makes a new decision every day. Whatever is best for her that day is what she goes with. As soon as I would have taken her in hand, she would have freaked out and ran back to Spencer."

"Are you willing to bet your life on that?" Anne chimes back in.

"I'm not willing to bet anything on her. Now please, guys, just leave me be." I stand and once again leave my family. I don't go to my room. There's too much of Quinn in there. The look on her face when she arrived, the crying in the bathroom...

I head out of the French doors and down to the beach. I can hear someone walking behind me. I don't have to look. I know it's Phil. He didn't say a word with my family around, but I know he holds an earful on his tongue now that we're alone.

I sit on the beach and feel the damp sand between my fingers as I grab a fistful and watch it fall slowly from my hand. "Say it."

"Okay, I will. I think you've thrown away a great thing," he spits out, not sparing my feelings like my family might have.

I lift my chin. "Is that it?"

"No, Brett. That's far from *it*. You broke her heart. You embarrassed her in front of everyone she has grown to love. Stop me if I'm wrong, but it looks like they all love her, too. You, most of all."

"You don't know the way she played me, Phil. Every step I took, every turn I made, she pushed me back and twisted me until it almost broke me. Just when I had my hands on the trophy, she snatched it away. Then she had the nerve to expect graciousness," I laugh.

"She expected me to just welcome her back with open arms. I was supposed to expect something different from her this time. You know the definition of stupidity? I do! It's doing the same thing over and over again and expecting different results."

"Yeah, Brett, I know, but I could see the difference in her. I know you could, too. This needs to be fixed. That's all I'm going to say.

"Now, your family is planning the farewell Malibu dinner tonight. No one will bring it up again. Everyone has said his or her peace. The rest is up to you, but they want to know if you plan on coming."

I nod.

"Okay," he says, standing and brushing himself off. "Then get ready. You look like a mess."

My lips purse. Kick me when I'm down. Thanks, bud.

I go into the dressing room that leads to the bathroom. This is where Quinn cried. I picture her there now, dotting the mascara from under her eyes as the tears fall.

I close my eyes, placing my hands on the counter to steady myself. Brushing my teeth, I make a poor attempt at personal hygiene before concluding a shower needs to be in my future.

Turning the water on as hot as I can stand it, I crack open the beer I brought with me and let the water turn my skin red under the stream as I chug it down. I miss her.

I hate to admit that, and I'd never admit it to my family, but

I do. Dinner is tonight. Now, I think of our first dinner together here. She was so cute eating crab legs for the first time.

A small smirk quickly turns to a frown and some anxiety. I let her go. She's gone.

———

AT DINNER, I pick at my food. I fork through my corn and stab at my steak with a knife. I listen to meaningless talk between my parents, like every other time I've accompanied them on this trip.

They talk about what a nice time they had, comment on the weather, and spill over how delicious the food has been. Like I said, meaningless talk. No one pays me much attention, for which I'm grateful.

Before we leave, as my father is paying the check, our waitress, whom I've caught catching glimpses of me throughout the night, slips me a piece of paper as I walk out the door. I already know what it is. A family vacationing in Malibu—I have money. She knows it, and I'm almost positive it's her number.

She's attractive. Maybe she's even more attractive than Quinn to some men. She's thin, blond hair, crystal blue eyes, and a smile that could leave some men broke and sleep deprived within a few days, but I only have eyes for one woman.

I open the paper in the taxi, and there it is. "Call me" written at the top with a phone number and signed by a girl named Mindy, who apparently dots her I's with hearts. I roll my eyes and shove the paper in my pocket.

"Got some digits, huh?" Phil asks.

"Looks like it."

"She was a looker." He gives the girl a compliment, but I know what he's getting at. He's trying to feel me out about whether I'm going to call her or not. It's none of his business.

Maybe meeting other girls is what I need, and not at some meet and greet like speed dating with a lot of desperate women looking for love in all the wrong places. I'm flattered by this girl picking me over Phil, when I've seen the way women flock to him. He's always been the better looking of us, in my opinion.

When we get home, I go to my room to crash. I take everything from my pockets and take my pants off to relax, tossing them on the chair of the mirrored vanity in the dressing room. I lie in bed, staring at the ceiling for an hour before glancing back at the change mound with a small piece of paper atop it. The number.

Mindy is probably off by now. Why I am fighting this so hard? Don't you get back on a horse that throws you? This moment is my horse. It's time for me to saddle up.

I grab the paper off the dresser and ignore the childish heart that stares back at me and dial her number from my cell.

"What are you doing?" I hear from my door. Phil.

"I'm calling the waitress."

His hands drop to his sides. "Brett, you don't want to see that girl, and you know it."

"Phil, you don't know what I want. I need to get out of this house, away from my family, and there's a girl who wants to get to know me."

"There's a girl back in Manhattan who's probably in shambles over you right now."

"No, there's a girl in Manhattan who's probably in the arms of another man right now."

"Well, if she is, you put her there, and don't forget it."

"Dude," I say, "you need to relax."

"No. No, I don't think I do. I watched you ruin years of your life with Lisa, and now I see you flushing a perfect relationship down the toilet for some waitress you don't know."

"What part of that relationship was perfect, Phil? You've got to be kidding me."

"She's your match, Brett. You know she is." I push him from my room and shut the door and hear him bang on the back of the door hard with his fist once before stomping back off to his room. I finish dialing Mindy's number.

"Hello?"

"Hey. This is Brett. We met at your work tonight."

"Yeah. Yeah, I remember. I'm so glad you called."

"I just got home a little while ago. Do you want to maybe meet up for a drink?"

She immediately becomes excited. "Yes! I would love to!"

"Great, there's a bar next to your restaurant. I'll buy you a drink. Meet you there in an hour?"

"Sounds amazing. I'll see you then."

I call a cab and in ten minutes, it's sitting outside the house. I close my bedroom door and who is standing in the stairwell? Phil.

"You're making a mistake."

"Maybe, but it's mine to make," I say, walking right past him and out the door. The whole ride into town, I'm jittery. I tap my foot and bite at my nails, which I've never done before.

When I arrive at the bar, I pay the cab driver and stand outside the bar for another five minutes, stewing over what I'm doing.

I'm nervous. I'm honestly nervous. Not because this is a date, but because I know that if I go through with this, there's no turning back, but now I think of Quinn and what she might be doing.

Maybe she's on her sofa eating a pizza and watching late night TV, but then again, maybe she is with Spencer drinking wine and reconciling or maybe even in the throes of passion. The latter throws my mind into a tailspin, and I enter the bar.

She's already here. I see her as soon as I walk in. There's no missing someone so attractive. Her blond hair is no longer tied back in a bun. It hangs freely with curls at the bottom.

Her long legs are no longer covered by her work slacks. They're crossed sexily, bare from the hem of the short red dress she's wearing down. I walk toward her, but my legs are like jelly beneath me.

"You made it," she says.

"Yeah, here I am," I laugh nervously.

"I didn't know what you drink or I would have ordered you something," she says before holding her hand up in the air and signaling a waiter.

"I'll have a whiskey and cola" I tell him.

"Another Cosmo for me, please" she says.

"You got it," he responds.

"So, you here on vacation?"

I tilt my head. "Yeah. How'd you guess?"

She laughs. "I try not to listen in on my customers' conversations, but sometimes you just hear things."

I'm going out of my way not to stare into her eyes.

"So, how does a guy as handsome as you stay single for this long?"

I smirk. "I don't know. Just unlucky in love I guess. What about you?"

"Oh, my last boyfriend was a real piece of work..." She rattles on, but I barely listen. I'm here in body but not in mind. I can't even attempt to be charming right now.

It's taking everything in me just to sit still in this chair. When the waiter brings the drink, I guzzle it down like it's nothing but water. It's when the glass is empty, and I see through the bottom that I feel like I've been struck by lightning. Her purse.

"Thirsty?" she asks.

"Yeah, I guess so. Is that your purse?"

She seems confused for a moment but laughs. "Yeah, I just got it actually. Do you like it?"

"What kind of print is that on it?"

"It's giraffe, I think."

My heart flutters. I can't do this. I grab for my wallet and pull a couple twenties out, tossing them on the table.

"I'm sorry. I have to go. Something suddenly came up."

"Came up? What are you talking about?" she asks frantically.

"I'm sorry," I say, rushing out the door and hailing a cab. I quickly give the driver the address to the beach house.

Once I arrive, I bang on Phil's door. "Phil! Phil!" I say pounding the door. He answers with groggy eyes. "Get packed. We're leaving. Tonight."

"Yes!" he says, turning back toward his room and grabbing random clothes.

I pack faster than I ever have before, making sure to only grab the necessities. Screw the rest. You never leave a woman waiting.

28

QUINN

SOON THOMAS and Fran rinse out their paint rollers and brushes, finish their glasses of wine, and help me put Evie to bed. By the time Fran says her goodbyes to Thomas and me, I'm exhausted. Thomas has yet to say his goodbyes, and I'm worried where any conversation between us will lead. I don't have to worry for long. He gets right to the point as I pour myself another glass of wine in the kitchen.

"Quinn, you know we need to talk."

"Thomas, I'm too tired to talk. I can't even begin to explain the week I've had."

"Oh, but I do. You were busy falling in love. Love can be tiring. I know from personal experience."

I slam the bottle of wine back on the counter and turn my back to him to take my first gulp from the glass.

"Thomas, I can't—"

"I know. I'm not here to give you a hard time." He joins me in the kitchen and pours himself another glass of wine. A bad sign. He plans to be here for a while.

He takes a sip and places the glass gingerly on the counter

before taking mine and doing the same. He takes my hands in his, and I can't look him in the eye.

"I'm here to say it's okay. I know all too well that you can't help who you love." He lowers his head and drops my hands gently. "All too well."

There's a pain in my chest.

"Thomas," I say, taking him in my arms. I hug him tightly. "I'll always love you. You and Fran are my truest friends."

"That's only because you're such a jerk," he jokes. I laugh, and I feel his body vibrate with a chuckle. "I've got to go." He hugs me tighter for only a moment before swallowing the last of his wine and opening the door.

I'm not prepared at all for what stands on the other side of the door. Holding his hand up, just about to knock, is Spencer. Thomas glances back at me and offers me a knowing eye.

"Spencer," he says.

"Thomas," Spencer offers in return.

Then Thomas is out of the door and I watch him disappear around the corner.

"I thought we agreed on tomorrow," I tell Spencer before walking back inside the house and leaving the door open for him.

"I know, but I couldn't wait."

"Spencer, it's just a bad time. You know, Evie is in bed, I just got home, I've been painting since I got here—"

He holds up his hand. "I know, but, uh, I just needed to see you. I miss you, Quinn."

I shake my head. "Do you miss me because Melissa left you?"

"Melissa didn't leave anyone. We were always fighting—"

"So *that's* why you guys split," I gather.

"We split because she wasn't you, Quinn. I never wanted to hurt you to begin with, and when you left, I had no one."

"So now you have no one, and you want me back."

"It's not like that," he says. "I want you back because I love you. I'm a grown man. I know how to be alone, and if I have to be alone, then so be it, but I would rather spend my life with you. Please, Quinn, don't let a stupid mistake I made ruin what could have been... what still can be."

I slump in a chair now. Maybe I can't be alone either.

Maybe I'm not strong enough, because the more he talks, the more I just want to curl up with him and forgive him. Or maybe I just want to curl up with *someone*.

"Please, Quinn, think of Evie. I don't want our child to come from a broken home. I know you don't either. Let's give her the family she deserves."

I sip my wine and sift through everything he says in my head.

Everything he is selling is making sense. I *do* want Evie to have a happy family. I don't want her to come from a broken home. I want the best for my daughter, but is Spencer the best? He is her father. Who could be better?

I love Spencer despite his faults. I've made my fair share of mistakes in this life, but I can't fail my daughter. Maybe he's seen the error of his ways.

"Just give me a chance. I'll agree to anything," he says.

A light bulb turns on. There's nothing wrong with giving someone a second chance.

"Okay," I sigh.

"Okay?" he says excitedly, exhaling a breath and kneeling in front of me now.

"You have to agree to something for me first."

"Anything."

"You can stay tonight, and we can talk more. When Evie wakes up in the morning, I don't want her to know you stayed here. I don't want to give her any false hopes if this doesn't work out."

"How long will we have to lie like this? I want you forever, Quinn."

"I'll know when the time is right to tell her."

The rest of the night, we talk. It doesn't take us long to cuddle up to one another on the couch. I'm enamored again by the man who made me fall for him so long ago. He's charming and makes me laugh, and soon I forgive his faults and lay my head on his chest.

His arm finds its way around me, and I'm torn between feeling safe and feeling confused. It was all just a bad dream. A nightmare. A mistake that was made that could have just as easily been my mistake.

This is the way my life is supposed to be. I'm supposed to be with Spencer and Evie as a family. There's a lapse in conversation, and his hand travels down to my waist.

I stare up at him and soon his lips are on mine. They feel odd, not like I remember. I remember feeling safe and protected before. This is a different sensation—as though I'm being duped, but I ignore it, and my hand finds his face.

His face is familiar. His skin is warm under my hand, and I run my fingers over his dark, freshly groomed beard. I'm more relaxed now. This is all coming back to me.

I love this man. He feels like home to me. I can be with him again.

Slowly we stand. I pull his shirt over his head, and he mirrors my move. We make our way to the bedroom where we kiss heavily.

"I love you so much," he says.

"I love you, too," and I mean it. I love him. I've always loved him and always will. He's the father of my child, and I've been with him for years and years.

Still, I don't think I can do this. Not yet. As we roll around on the bed, I stop him.

"Wait. Wait," I say, pushing him away as he tries to kiss my neck.

"What is it? What's wrong?"

"I can't. I just can't, yet. It's too soon, and I'm not sure of anything. I can't get in this deep right now."

He takes a long, hard breath and sits up on the bed. "Quinn, it's still me, and I love you."

"If that's the case, then you can wait for me. I'm not ready for this, yet."

I see his cheek flex where he grinds his teeth. "There's someone else." I shake my head. "Who did you go to Malibu with?"

"I went with Fran." Truth.

"Who else was there?"

"Spencer, that's none of your business. You were shacked up with a stripper at the time!" I stand and grab a shirt from the dresser. He comes up behind me and kisses my bare shoulder before I put it on.

"I know. It's none of my business. I'm sorry. I'm just wanting to know what I'm up against here."

"You're not up against anyone but yourself, Spencer." I put the shirt on and grab a pillow and blanket from the linen closet, leaving the bedroom and tossing them on the sofa. "This is where you sleep tonight."

"On the couch?"

"Yes, on the couch. Is that a problem?"

He throws his hands up. "No. No problem. Whatever you want. I don't want to rush you."

He turns the television on low, and I creep back to my room, stealing a peak of Evie through her cracked door on my way. I lie in bed and listen to the low TV from my bedroom. I can't tell what he's watching, but I let the noise lull me into a deep sleep.

I awake the next morning to an unfamiliar sound. My eyes open, and I squint against the sun trickling through the blinds. I push against the light with my hand and search for the source of the sound. There, wrapped up in my blanket, is a phone. It's not mine. It has to be Spencer's.

"One new message" it says. I glance toward my door. On the other side of it is Spencer, maybe still asleep. I swipe the phone open. It's from Melissa. "Where are you?" it says.

Why does Melissa want to know where Spencer is? He left her. Didn't he?

He didn't. He still has her on the hook, or maybe he's just keeping *me* on the hook. I storm into the living room and yank the pillow from under his head. His head plops on the couch cushion beneath him.

"Hey! What's the big deal?"

"I could ask you the same question," I say, tossing the phone on his chest. "Why does Melissa want to know where you are? Are you late for a date or something?"

"Baby—"

"Don't 'Baby' me, Spencer."

"Would you just listen? I don't know why she's asking me. Maybe she went back to my house looking for me. The point is, she didn't find me there because I'm with you," he says, taking my hands in his. "Because I'm here with you," he says again in a calm voice.

Confusion once again.

29

BRETT

THIS PLANE RIDE has taken forever, and it's taking even longer for everyone to file off. I can't wait to see Quinn, and I can only hope she hasn't done something crazy like take her ex back. I hope.

Janine is supposed to be picking Phil and me up here at the airport and giving us a ride back home. Not my first choice, but Kara was busy, and obviously, the rest of my family is in Malibu. When they learned I was running back to Manhattan to win Quinn back, they were all quite excited.

Each one took me off to the side to give me his or her own individual pep talk. Even my father, though he didn't say much, told me he was proud of me, and that was enough.

"I'm so happy you finally came to your senses," Phil says as we stand to exit the plane.

"I just hope this isn't another mistake on my part."

"Hey," he claps my shoulder, "no matter what happens, this isn't a mistake. It's never a mistake to go after the woman you love."

"I hope you're right."

"You hope? When have I ever steered you wrong?" he laughs.

"Oh, I could name a few times."

He laughs. "Name one."

"How about the night you got me liquored up and had me dive off the roof and into the pool of the local fraternity house?"

He laughs hysterically. "Okay, first, you got yourself liquored up, and secondly, that was the greatest thing I had ever seen!"

"Do we even remember why we went there?" I ask, laughing.

"Err... nope."

I chuckle.

We walk quickly through the airport and out the front doors to see Janine propped up against her car, looking cuter than ever, waiting on us. Phil and I wave, and she gives us a huge smile.

"So, how was the trip? You're home early," she says as we climb into the car, luggage first.

"The trip was amazing!" Phil answers.

"Phil fell in love," I say.

"*Phil?*" she asks.

"Yup, head over heels. I think he's ready to put down some roots."

"Okay, first, don't talk about me like I'm not here, and second, I haven't mentioned any kind of roots."

"What about you, Brett? You fall in love, too?" she asks.

"I don't think this is the right time ..." my voice trails off.

She stares at me solemnly through the rearview mirror. She drops Phil off at his apartment, and I move into the front seat, not because I want to, but because I don't want Janine feeling like a limo driver.

The talk between us is minimal during the ride to my apartment. It's awkward, and I'm wishing she had dropped me off before Phil. She drives slowly, as though she's not ready for us to part. When the car finally stops in front of my building, I fight the urge to jump out immediately and head to Quinn. I know I can't do that.

"You came home early for her, didn't you?" she asks.

"Janine—"

"I'm not here to give you a hard time, Brett," she interrupts. "I just want you to know you have other options. I'm sitting right here in front of you, and I could love you if you would just let me."

"Janine, I care about you, but only as a friend."

"If you would just give me a chance, you might feel differently. I know I'm a little younger, but I hear some guys dig that," she jokes, yet I'm almost certain she's serious.

I laugh. "Yeah, I suppose some guys do, but your age isn't a problem." I suck in a breath deeply, exhaling loudly. "The problem is I am in love with someone else."

"How could you love someone who makes you so insane and brushes you off half the time? Yeah, Phil filled us all in over the past week. Seems like he called us at the bar every day you were gone."

I roll my eyes. "Janine, do you think you love me?"

"Yes."

"How can you love me when I make you so insane and brush you off half the time?" I raise my eyebrows at her. "Hmm?"

She smirks. "I don't like your reasoning."

I laugh and take her hand. "I'm sorry, Janine, but I'm just not the guy for you."

"She's a lucky girl. I hope she realizes that."

"I hope she does, too." I pat her hand before exiting the car, grabbing my bag, and watching her drive away. Maybe, finally, she understands.

Exhausted, I open the door to the apartment building and drag my bag behind me. All I want is a hot shower, fresh clothes, and to find Quinn.

I finally make it to the shower. I barely feel the water on my skin at all. I want to feel cleansed of everything, but it's not working. The motivation I had last night has dwindled and I feel terrified now. In a strange way, Quinn scares me.

She has a power over me that I don't understand. After just two weeks, I'm ready to give up my bachelor life and dive head-first into a relationship with her. Will she still be ready to do that with me?

I wash myself robotically, closing my eyes against the stream of water and trying to decide what my plan of action is. Do I call her first? What if she won't hear me out? Do I show up on her doorstep, hoping she will let me in? Or do the rules still apply?

We've broken so many of them at this point that I'm not sure if rules are even a part of our relationship anymore. She has me completely vulnerable.

I dress comfortably and decide to go to my bar first to check on things. Maybe I will have a little well-deserved talk with Kara.

I walk the streets of Manhattan slowly, happy to be back home and enjoying the autumn weather. I walk slowly. Not because I'm carelessly strolling, but because I have to get my bearings about me. A useless notion.

When I arrive at the bar, Kara is wiping down the counter and Phil is having a drink. He must have come straight from home to the bar.

"So, how did it go?" Kara asks with a smirk.

I chuckle. "Like Phil hasn't already filled you in."

"Yeah, he has, and if memory serves, you're supposed to be sweeping a girl off her feet right about now."

"Yeah. I'm working up to it."

"I wouldn't wait too long if I were you," she says.

30

QUINN

"THIS IS what I'm talking about, Spencer. I can't trust you!"

"You can, Quinn! Let me prove it to you."

For the past hour, Spencer and I have been arguing over his text from Melissa. I think he is hiding something, but he promises he's not. He says Melissa's sending him a text means nothing. I'm so glad Evie is still asleep.

"How? How do you plan to prove it?"

"I'll let you talk to her," he says. "Face to face. You can ask her anything you want. I have nothing to hide."

Now there's an idea. I've wanted a sit down with Melissa for quite some time now. This is an open invitation to ask her why she can't find a family of her own rather than stealing another's.

"Fine. I'll take you up on that," I say. I grab my scarf and coat, and he gulps before grabbing his own. I know this isn't the perfect scenario for him, but if he truly has nothing to hide, then he has nothing to worry about.

"What about Evie?" he asks.

"We will drop her off at Fran's on the way."

We take Spencer's car across Manhattan and drop Evie off

at Fran's. Evie is always so excited to see her Aunt Fran. I'm blessed that my child loves my friends.

Then we head to wherever Melissa is hanging her hat. We pass the cutoff for Spencer's place, so I know immediately that she's not there. That's a good sign. Soon we are pulling up to a strip club.

Oh, *that's* why she isn't at Spencer's house. She's at work. Perfect. Just perfect.

Spencer strolls into The Gentleman's Club as if he's been there a hundred times. Probably because he has. I creep in behind him, afraid someone will recognize me. I walk where he walks and don't touch a thing.

"Wait here," he says, placing me at a table. "I'll be back in a second." I watch him go up to a man posted outside a door that I can only imagine leads to the dressing room for the girls since it says, "Staff Only."

Regardless, I see Spencer clap the guy on the shoulder and motion for me to join him. I do, and we enter the dressing room with numerous girls getting ready for their turn on stage. There are platform heels, leather bras, and thong underwear. Most everything in the room can only be found online or at sex shops.

"Here she is," Spencer mutters.

Melissa is so young. I knew she was only twenty-one, but looking at her now, she looks like a kid. She's tall, with long black hair and bronzed skin. Her eyes are a piercing black to match her dark hair. This is the first time we've been properly introduced.

"Melissa, Quinn wishes to speak with you."

"Alone," I add.

"Sorry," she says. "I'm at work and don't have time for this."

"Spencer if she's not willing to talk—"

"Oh, I'm willing," she interrupts, "but my time is worth

money. We can talk, but you'll pay for me like any other customer would."

I glance at Spencer. It's taking everything in me not to yank this young girl up and put her over my knee like the toddler she is.

"I'll pay for it," Spencer huffs, whipping his wallet out of his back pocket and handing her a twenty-dollar bill.

She snatches the twenty from his hand. "Come with me."

I assume Spencer is going to wait in the main room where the strippers are working. Great. This time it's me bringing him here, and with the way life has been going, I'm not surprised.

We enter a room only hidden by a pink curtain of sorts, and inside is only a couch with a small table holding a dim lamp beside it and music is playing through a speaker.

"I guess I don't have to ask what goes on in here," I say.

"I'm not a slut, Quinn. We give lap dances in this room, and I can promise you I work harder for a buck than you ever have."

"Yeah, I bet."

"What are you two doing here? What do you want from me?"

"I want to know what went down with you and Spencer."

"When and why?"

"From start to finish would be nice because now he's saying he wants to come home."

She laughs. "Why am I not surprised? Look, you don't have anything to worry about. Spencer and I are a thing of the past."

"How... how long were you seeing my husband before I found out?" I choke the words out. They sting my throat as they exit.

Her stern face now softens just slightly. Had I not seen it happen, I would not have known. "A while."

"A while?"

She sighs. "Spencer started coming in here a few years ago. We started seeing one another a year before you separated."

I shake my head. "You knew he was married. He had a daughter at home."

"Yeah, I knew that, but as the saying goes, you can't help who you love."

"So, you do love him?"

"No. I loved what he stood for—family, work, a sense of normalcy in this world. He had everything I wanted, and he was willing to give it to me. I stopped showing my body for every man who threw a dollar bill my way. I had a life with him. I could have had children and gone to the grocery store without seeing my customers with their wives and kids and feeling like the scum of the earth."

"You could have gotten those things for yourself, not stolen them from another woman."

"I did get those things for myself, Quinn, but obviously, no woman can compete with you."

"Meaning?" I ask.

"I knew he never loved me. Just like I did with him, he saw something in me that he thought he wanted. Maybe youth or just the kinky thought of sleeping with a stripper. We never saw one another for what we truly were. We only liked the idea of one another.

"Soon the illusion was shattered. I started acting like a wife, and I could tell if he wanted a wife, it would be you. We tried to make it work. I offered to become a part of Evie's life, and he never brought you up, but we both knew the truth."

"What's that?"

"That it was never going to work. That we didn't love each other."

"Then why did you text him last night?"

212

She sucks in a breath. "He told me he was going to try to reconcile with you, but if he couldn't, he said he'd give me an honest chance. Not like before. I would give him an honest chance, too. I assume since you're here, I've lost my chance."

"Melissa, you were okay with that?" I ask. "Being put on the back burner? To come in second to another woman?"

"There are not many options for people like me, Quinn. I'm a nobody. I have no family. I have no job skills. My only friends are strippers, too. Sure, I can turn some heads, but what respectable man would ever want to marry a stripper? I can't think of one. Spencer might have wanted to if you didn't take him back. So yeah, I was okay with coming in second."

Every woman is worth something, but here stands Melissa, who only wants a normal life and doesn't think she is good enough to have it. She doesn't see that her job doesn't define her. Suddenly I feel sorry for this young girl. Every shield I built up for this moment has crumbled, and like the mother I am, I see a child, a child who aches for something she has never had: a family. Such a simple request, and for a moment I wonder if I were in her shoes, would I have done the same?

"Do you trust him?" she asks, tearing me away from my thoughts.

"I want to."

She shakes her head. "After everything?"

"You were willing to be with him," I snap, "despite the fact he loved me."

She chuckles sarcastically. "I don't have the options you have. It made him crazy, you know."

"What did?"

"Your being gone. Come on, one woman to another. You were with another man, weren't you?"

"What if I was?"

"It made him crazy with jealousy. I dance naked for a

213

hundred men a night, and he doesn't get jealous. He doesn't say a word. He watches me come to this room where he knows I'm giving lap dances, and yet he said nothing the whole first year we saw one another.

"You go to the beach with a boyfriend, and it might as well have been front page news in our house. If you have another man, and this man is good to you, then why come back to a man who left you for someone like me? Or maybe... maybe you're even more screwed up than I am."

She stares at me in a pitiful way. I had stared at her the same way only a moment ago. Two broken women who might have made good friends if not for this disaster. We peer at one another with fresh eyes, as if seeing each other for the first time. I duck my eyes away from her, afraid she can see through to my broken soul.

"It's okay," she says. "You have choices, something not everyone has. Make the right one." She squeezes past me and walks from the room, leaving me in the dark with way too many thoughts.

Can I trust him? I want to so badly. I want to go back to the time when things made sense and I was ignorantly happy. This all seems like such a bad dream.

I find Spencer. "How'd it go?" he asks.

"I found the answers I was looking for."

"Good," he says, putting his arm around me as we leave. Suddenly I feel dirty. His arm around me no longer is a safe place. It feels foreign. Maybe I don't know him at all.

Spencer says he wants to take me to a restaurant, since Fran is already watching Evie for us. I agree, though I'm hesitant. He takes me to the Italian restaurant where I had Brett and Phil meet me that first day, which seems like so long ago now.

We sit at a booth across from where Brett and I sat, right next to a window, and I can't help but catch glimpses of the couple sitting at the other booth now. Little candles sit on the table with a white tablecloth, and they hold hands across the table.

"Do you know them?" Spencer asks before ordering us drinks.

"No. They just remind me of a couple I used to know." Were we ever a couple though? I suppose there's just no other way to describe what we were. We weren't friends, although some days it felt like it. We weren't engaged, although we pretended, and we weren't married, although now as I watch the other couple, I think of how wonderful it might be to be married to Brett.

The waitress brings us each a glass of red wine, and we order from the menu. I choose the first thing I see, which is spaghetti with meat sauce, and I can't even recall what Spencer ordered. As the waitress walks off, I catch a glimpse of Spencer. He's staring at something. I follow his eyes.

Her butt. He's literally staring at our waitress's butt as she walks off. It's as though I've been struck by lightning, and everything suddenly makes sense. He will never change. I'll always have to worry about where he is when he is five minutes late, or what that unusual smell is on his clothes, or who sent him a text early in the morning.

I can't live my life like that. I glance to the other couple again who are still holding hands across the table. I know where I'm supposed to be, and it's not here with him.

"I have to go."

"Go? Where are we going?"

"*We* are not going anywhere. I'm going. I can't do this with you. I can't go back to you, Spencer. I'm sorry." I'm not sorry though. I finally know what I want. Or rather, who.

31

BRETT

I TAKE Kara's words to heart. I can't leave Quinn waiting. The last thing I want is for her to run back to Spencer because I was the dummy who sent her away. I shake my head at my own stupidity. What was I thinking?

I needed her love, and when she finally came to declare it, I pushed her away. I was scared. Every time I'd take that step forward, I was reminded just how broken she was. She would always push me back.

I take the time to finish my beer with Phil and Kara. A little liquid courage never hurt anyone, right? Soon the time comes when I know I must make my move. I gather the strength to stand and say goodbye to Phil and Kara. I straighten my jacket and smooth back my hair.

This is it. My whole life has led me to this one point in time. I'm supposed to be with Quinn. She realized it, and now so have I. I set off on foot.

I decide to walk because I need to pick something up for her. Flowers, maybe? You don't show up announcing your love for someone and asking for forgiveness for being a dope without some kind of token. I enter a small gift shop on the corner and skim the aisles.

I check out all the little trinkets on the glass shelves. I feel fake flowers and see cute coffee mugs and cards. There would never be a card that described our situation. I chuckle to myself at the thought of what our card would say.

I laugh to myself in the aisle, and the laugh doesn't go unnoticed by an elderly woman nearby. I nod politely, still amused, and I walk past her, chuckling again at the look of suspicion on her face. She probably thinks I'm crazy. I'm starting to think so, too.

I finally stumble upon a shelf filled with stuffed animals, and I hold my breath. There. There it is. I grab it up and check out quickly. No apology card needed. I don't think showing up with something like flowers or jewelry would be Quinn's style. I have the perfect gift, I'm sure of it.

I mosey through the streets, headed straight for Quinn's house now. No more pit stops, no more distractions. I know exactly what I intend to say, and I can't see Quinn turning me down. I hold my head up high in the sky, and there's a little pep in my step.

It isn't until I pass our Italian restaurant that I'm stopped in my tracks. It isn't because I'm reminiscing, though I wish it was. I see her. I see my beautiful Quinn, but she's not alone. Sitting across from her is another man, and I'd bet money it's Spencer.

My heart sinks deep into my soul as I see her staring at him. She's not smiling, but that doesn't tell me anything. I glance down at the sack in my hand. I consider dropping it in the street right now and running in the opposite direction. A serious consideration.

Instead, I stand there and stare for what seems like hours. She doesn't see me, and neither does he, though he wouldn't know who I was. I'm just some guy staring at his wife.

She went through with it. She took him back. That can be the only reason they are together so intimately right now.

I dial Phil's number.

"Where are you?" I ask.

"Just got home. Why?"

"We need to talk. Can I come over?"

"Yeah, bud. I'm here."

I hang up the phone without so much as a goodbye. It takes every ounce of my being to turn and walk away from this scene instead of spying on her. Creeping isn't my style. I head for Phil's condo instead.

When I walk in a short time later, it's just as it has always been. Pool table where a dining table should be, empty beer bottles on every surface, unmade bed just a room away. A stereotypical bachelor's pad. Phil is on the couch watching television when I walk in.

I didn't bother knocking. He never knocks on my door either. We've always been more like family, and neither of us has anything to hide. Besides, he knew I was coming.

"What's going on?" he asks, setting yet another empty bottle on the makeshift coffee table.

"I saw Quinn."

He stares at me, ready for more, but that's all I can manage to choke out.

"I take it since you're here and not there that it didn't go well. I'm sorry, man. Sit down."

"It didn't go anywhere at all. I was walking to her house, and I saw her at that Italian restaurant with a man."

"Was it her ex-husband?"

"I can only assume."

"Crap."

"Yeah. You think Fran will know what's going on? Has she mentioned anything to you?" I ask desperately.

"Not a thing, but I can call her."

"Yeah, do that."

As he dials her number; I go to his kitchen for a beer of my own, fighting the urge to sit beside him and hog the ear piece like a school girl. I stay in the kitchen with my back toward him, listening to a lot of "Oh, yeah?" and "Uh-huh" coming from Phil.

Finally, I can't wait any longer. "What's she doing with him?" I storm back into the room.

He stares up at me from his seated position. "Maybe you should talk to her," he says, handing me the phone.

I snatch it from his hands. "Fran, talk to me."

"She decided to give him another chance, Brett. You left her high and dry. You embarrassed her. She came back for you."

I sink into the couch, and my head falls in my hands. "I know. I know." I sigh.

"Look, I think you still have a chance here. Quinn will find out soon enough that Spencer will never change, and I know how she feels about you."

"How does she feel, Fran? What was she going to tell me when you guys came back?"

She hesitates. "I can't tell you everything, but she was going to tell you that she wanted to be with you. I know Quinn, and the only reason she is even giving Spencer another chance is because you failed her. I hate to put it that way, but you did. You dropped the ball big time."

I shake my head. Yes, I dropped the ball. I still say it could have gone fifty-fifty though. She might have run off scared the next day.

"I think this actually goes in your favor, Brett," she says.

"Well, I'd sure love for you to explain that one."

"In my opinion, all she's doing is giving him another chance to fail, and trust me, he will. He's a real piece of work. Then she will know for sure what she wants. There will be no more questions."

She has a point. I was thinking the other day that if she didn't give Spencer another chance, she would always wonder what would have happened, but how long do I wait for *him* to drop the ball?

"Thanks, Fran."

"Brett, wait."

I rub my head, not sure I can take in any new information she might want to offer. "What is it?"

"Don't wait for Spencer to mess up. Go to her. For all we know, that's what she's waiting on, for you to come to your senses. This is your life. You want her in it, don't you?"

I sigh deeply, a breath I had been holding in without realizing it. "More than anything."

"Then don't let that man stand in your way."

I feel a surge of electricity spiral through me at her words. She's right. I can't cower here like a whipped dog with my tail between my legs.

No one said life is easy. Sometimes you have to fight for what you want. I hang up the phone and stare across the room.

"What'd she say?" Phil asks, popping open another bottle.

"Exactly what I needed to hear."

I grab my jacket, which I don't even remember taking off, and the present and head for the door.

"What's in the bag?" Phil calls out after me.

"The ace up my sleeve."

32

QUINN

I CALL Fran and have her meet me with Evie at the coffee shop. When I see Evie, I know I've done the right thing. My daughter deserves better. I wouldn't be happy with Spencer, and Evie deserves a happy mother.

Fran is all smiles, and I'm happy to see a smiling face.

"You seem happy," I tell her.

"You do, too," she says.

I grin at her. "I am happy."

"Happy with Spencer?" she asks with a cocked head.

Evie swings from our hands, paying no attention to our conversation as she squeals in delight.

I laugh through my nose and shake my head. "Happy without him."

"Oh, thank goodness! Does this mean you're going to go after Brett?"

"No. As much as I love Brett, there's just too much about my life he doesn't know." I motion to Evie.

"He would understand."

I shake my head so lightly that I'm not sure if it's noticeable. "I've done too much to him. He probably felt like a yo-yo the way I played with him. I can't drag him into my messed-up life. He deserves better."

"You're wrong. After everything you put him through, he deserves *you*."

"Thanks, Fran, but we're okay."

She nods. "I know." We kiss one another on the cheek, and I watch her cross the street safely. I head inside to get a quick coffee to go.

On the way home, Evie tells me all about her and Fran doing arts and crafts and pulls a card from her bag that she made for me. It's red construction paper with pink hearts that are also made from construction paper, and inside she drew the two of us as stick figures holding hands. It brings a tear to my eye. Not long ago, she would have drawn a whole family.

"Thank you, sweetie. This will go right on the fridge for everyone to see," I tell her with a kiss. She giggles and hugs my neck.

When we arrive home, I toss my house key in the bowl next to the door and tell Evie we can finish painting her room, which thrills her. I give her a simple paintbrush with green paint and get her started before I begin drawing another oversized red blob on the wall—the start of yet another ladybug—but it isn't long before I hear a knock at the door.

I know it can't be Spencer—he'd be crazy to come here. Fran was on her way home. It can only be Thomas. I sigh.

Things have just gotten too awkward between Thomas and me. Although he apologized and we moved past discussing his love, it will always be the elephant in the room. I drop the paint-brush and tell Evie to stay in her room. I am set on telling him I'm not in the mood for company, and I don't want Evie to see him and ask him to help.

I unlock the door with a roll of my eyes and open it. My breathing halts.

"Brett?"

"Hello, Quinn."

I quickly shut the door behind me and push my way outside with him. "What are you doing here?"

He shakes his head. "I know you're giving your ex a second chance, and I understand why but—"

"No, I'm not."

"You're not?"

"No. I mean, I was going to but... I just couldn't go through with it. I can't be with someone I can't trust."

His eyes show signs of relief and hope. "Can you trust me?"

My heart slightly leaps in my chest. This is what I had wanted only days before, and I do trust him, but he would never trust me after he found out I have a daughter.

"Yes, I can trust you, but you can't trust me."

His head tilts to the side and his body all but deflates where he stands. "What do you—"

"Momma," my daughter's sweet voice calls from the now open door. I glance to Brett's face and shock spreads across it. He stares from Evie back to me.

"Momma is talking to a friend right now, baby. Go back inside. I'll be back in there in a minute."

Evie eyes the stranger outside the door but complies.

I suck in a deep breath before hesitantly turning to Brett.

"You have a daughter," he says.

I nod and cross my arms—not in anger, but in an attempt to protect myself from whatever comes next.

"Why didn't you ever tell me?"

I shrug slightly and stare down, finding it increasingly hard to meet his eyes. "You were just supposed to be a fling, Brett. I never imagined..." The silence becomes deafening.

His arms hang long at his sides, and he stares down at the bag in his hands. "I got you something, if you want it."

My eyes find the bag.

I know now what people mean when they say you can cut the tension with a knife it's so thick. "Sure."

He reaches into the bag and pulls out a stuffed giraffe. I lean my head back to stifle the tears in my eyes. He hands me the giraffe, and I hold it close to my chest.

"Everything makes so much more sense now," he says. "Why you were so torn, why you wanted to give Spencer another chance, why every time I reached for you, you'd pull away."

"I never meant to hurt you. I just didn't want a stranger knowing everything about me. I love my daughter more than life itself, and I just wanted to protect her from what I was doing—speed dating, meeting up with a strange man for sex, going to Malibu with said stranger."

He nods quickly. "You came back that day to tell me about her, didn't you?"

"I came back to tell you a lot."

"Well, I'm here now. You can tell me."

"It doesn't matter anymore. I've lied to you, kept things from you, and you were right to send me away. I would have sent me away, too."

He nods. "I *was* right to send you away because now you know Spencer isn't the man for you. You never would have found that out if I hadn't. You would have lived with doubt, and I couldn't have that, but I'm here now. I'm right here, Quinn, and I don't want to be anywhere else."

"You said everything is so tainted, Brett." I finally let a tear fall from my face, but I brush it away quickly.

"Nothing is tainted. This is how it was supposed to happen. Can't you see that? We were supposed to meet and fall in love, and you were supposed to find out that I'm the man for you. This is the only way that could have happened."

"I have a daughter, Brett. I have an eight-year-old."

He shakes his head. "You say that like it's a problem."

I finally meet his eyes.

"It's not a problem, Quinn. A child is a blessing, and if she's anything like you, I'll love her one day, too, if you let me."

I cover my eyes with my hand. He's always known exactly what to say and do. Exactly. It's frustratingly beautiful. I had counted on him getting angry and storming off, but I should have known he would be as understanding as he's always been.

"Quinn, I'm not looking to marry you right now. As it is right now, I'm just looking to be with you and meet this beautiful eight-year-old in your house. I'm not rushing you into anything. Let me be here. Let me do this."

I hang my head and wipe tears away. I give myself a moment for composure. Then I peer up and search his waiting eyes. A laugh of exhaustion escapes me. "Do you like to paint?"

He smiles a crooked smile. "I'm a painter from way back."

33

BRETT

QUINN INTRODUCES me to her daughter, and she is the spitting image of her mother. It's almost as though I'm catching a glimpse of what Quinn looked like as a child.

"Evie, this is my friend Brett. Can you say hi?"

"Hi, Brett!" she exclaims. "We're painting my room with ladybugs! Do you want to help?" Just like a child. She's never met a stranger. I'm sure, as a parent, that must be scary at times.

"I would love to help, Evie."

Evie lets out a giggle and skips to her room where there is green paint everywhere, and I'm sure her mother is thankful for the protective plastic I see on the floor.

"So, you like giraffes, and she likes ladybugs," I comment.

She nods. "Since she was little everyone has called her 'Bug' and has given her ladybug toys and pictures, so it all just kind of fell into place that way."

"What about you, Mom?"

"What about me?"

"Why do you love giraffes?"

"Evie," she calls out to her. "Brett and I are going to be in the living room for a few minutes, okay?"

"Okay, Momma!" she exclaims.

She goes into the kitchen and retrieves two glasses and a bottle of wine and brings them into the living area. "Why do I like giraffes?" she repeats. We sit on the couch, and she pours us each a glass from the bottle. "Because it reminds me of the only time I can remember when life made sense."

She leans back on the couch, and I position my body to face her with my arm comfortably placed on the back of the sofa.

"When I was a little girl, I used to love to go to the zoo. I loved animals, and it became a monthly thing that my dad would take me to the zoo. He and my brother Randy would go fishing, but I always wanted to go to the zoo.

"So once a month, my father would take me. My favorite thing in the world was to watch the giraffes eat from the tops of the trees. We would stand there with our snow cones and watch the giraffes for the majority of the visit.

"Each time we would go, he would stop at the gift shop there and buy me some sort of giraffe—a stuffed animal, a trinket, a statue." Her voice trails off as she remembers. At first, she seemed to enjoy telling this story, but now it seems hard to choke out.

"Then one day my mother told me that my dad wasn't coming home. I would wait by my window, convinced that if I prayed hard enough that I would see his truck pull up, but days turned into weeks, weeks turned into months, and soon after, months turned into years.

"All I had left of my dad were the giraffes. When I turned into a teenager, I thought seriously about throwing them all out. By then I had learned that he left us all to be with another woman and another family. I still don't know how he was able to do that. I stare at Evie and can't imagine a life without her, but I kept them all because they reminded me of a time when I was at my happiest. My most carefree.

"I haven't felt that way since my father left. Then I grew up and lost my mother. All I had of either of them were the giraffes and the memories."

I take her hand in mine, and she leans her head over to peer at me. "Your life will make sense again. I promise."

She barely acknowledges my statement, as though she's heard those words before, and I duck my head.

She was right. There's so much about her I still don't know, but everything I hear about her only makes me love her more. My heart goes out to her, and I hate her father for taking away such a beautiful woman's spirit at such a young age. I pray to her mother to help me give her what she needs in this life.

Quinn pats my leg sternly. "Let's paint. If we are lucky, with your help, we can have this finished by tonight."

I clap my hands. "Let's get to it then."

———

THE REST OF THE DAY, Evie dominates the conversation, but I love it. It's so carefree. She tells me all about how her nickname is Bug and how she wants me to help her paint the grass while her mother finishes the bugs. I catch a glimpse of what Quinn must have been like at that age before her father left.

She laughs and paints, and I dot her nose with the paintbrush, which makes her laugh harder as she smears my favorite shirt with more green paint, but I don't care. I'm having the time of my life with these two ladies, and I thank Spencer for breaking her heart.

If he hadn't, I wouldn't have the chance to take care of her. I wouldn't enjoy her hugs or her kisses or her laughter. I thank all the men who broke her heart because it led her to me.

I thank every man who didn't kiss her because it left her lips open to me. I thank every man for walking away without hugging her because it left her arms open for me. In all that I've done in my life, this makes the most sense.

I finally see what it can be like for her and for myself. I could have a family. I never felt like I could have a family with Lisa. She never wanted children. I always prayed she would change her mind, but now I see that people like Lisa aren't built for children.

———

WE FINISH the room around eight-thirty, and by this time, Evie and I are old friends. She even asks Quinn if I can read her a bedtime story. She chooses one of my favorites from growing up.

Quinn is in the room with us as I read, sitting in a corner chair with a cute little smile on her face as Evie begins drifting in and out of sleep. When I hear her breathing become steady, I glance down to see she's asleep. Quinn winks at me, and I close the book as she tucks the covers under Evie's arms and kisses her forehead.

We quietly clean up the plastic from the floor and grab all the paintbrushes, pans, and rollers and admire the room. It's done. The walls have powder blue skies, white, fluffy clouds, floating ladybugs, and bright green grass. It's perfect. We shut her door, leaving her to dream.

In the kitchen, we rinse out all the rollers and pans in comfortable silence, both of us smiling for probably different reasons, but perhaps the same. When we finally plop down on the couch, all I can think of is that I want this to be my life forever. I want the house, and the children, and most of all, I want Quinn.

"It's getting late. Should I go?"

She shrugs. "Do you have a curfew?"

I chuckle. "No, I suppose not."

"Can I ask you something?" she says, changing the subject abruptly.

"Of course."

"Why did you come here today? I mean, why do you want this so much? Why do you want *me* when you could probably have anyone?"

I lower my eyes before staring back into hers. "Because when I met you, I saw someone as broken as I was."

"You never seemed broken."

I laugh. "I can hide it a lot better than you."

She grins. "Yeah, I suppose I didn't hide it well."

"It's okay. It's what drew me to you. You fascinated me. I could tell you weren't like the rest of the women in that room. I could tell you wanted more than they did."

"But I asked for less."

"Actions speak louder than words."

We sit in silence for a few minutes, sipping our wine, and I put my arm around her. "I love your daughter. She's amazing."

"She's everything I'm not. She's energetic, lovable, and trusting. I wish my life were as simple as wanting ladybugs on my bedroom walls."

"Well, what do you want?" I ask.

She flips her hair from her face. "Right now? Just this. I want my daughter safe in her room and the man I love with his arm around me."

I pull her in tighter. "Then that's what you'll get."

She stares up into my eyes. "I wouldn't mind a kiss though."

I glance down at her, and my eyes slowly close as my lips find hers. I've waited all day—no—I've waited my whole life for this kiss, and it's so much more than that. I can feel it.

It's the start of something new. No more secrets. No more

pulling away from one another. It's the start of a relationship. This time she actually said she loves me.

I couldn't ask for more than I have right now. I'm the luckiest man in the world. Unfortunately, this man has to go to work, and I still have to go to my house to change clothes first, having had a paint war with Evie. I smile at the memory.

Quinn walks me to the door. "So, what happens now?" she asks.

"Anything you want."

"I want to see you tomorrow."

"Then I guess you'll see me tomorrow. Why don't you have Evie ready around six tomorrow night? My family will be back, and I'd like them to meet her."

"I'd like that, too."

With a simple yet loving kiss goodbye, I set off for my apartment. Soon after I change clothes, I'm headed to the bar where I know Kara and Phil are both waiting for the day's details. I smile at the notion because I do want to tell someone—anyone— everyone about my day.

———

"THERE HE IS!" Phil exclaims as I walk through the door. "Did you get the girl?"

I laugh and clap his shoulder. "I got the girl."

Kara and Phil both whoop and holler. I tell them all about Quinn's and my exchange, and I tell them about Evie.

"You're going to love this kid, Phil. She's amazing."

"That's great, man. You've always wanted a family."

"A big one," I say from my bar stool.

Janine, having overheard the conversation, cracks open a beer and places it in front of me. "I'm happy for you, Brett." She seems genuine as she wipes down the bar and grabs another beer for a customer, walking out to the main floor.

"What's gotten into her?" I ask.

"Oh, she's got her eyes on a new prize," Kara says, motioning to a tall, dark gentleman Janine is now serving.

I raise my eyebrows. "That didn't take long."

"It never does at that age," Phil says.

An hour into the work night, Fran walks through the door of the bar. Phil jumps to his feet to offer her his chair, and we all sit around a table with a beer.

"So, have you talked to Quinn?" I ask.

"No. I came here to ask Phil how he thought it was going. I'm surprised you're here. So, how'd it go? Did you go to her?"

"I did. Fran, we had the most amazing night. I met Evie, so you don't have to keep that a secret anymore," I say, eying her.

She holds up her hands. "It wasn't my secret to tell."

I laugh. "I know. It's all okay."

"So, tell me everything," she says.

"Well, I met Evie, we finished painting her room, and then Quinn told me she loved me. We kissed goodnight, and I left. Yeah, that about sums it up."

Fran squeals. "She admitted to loving you?"

I nod with a cocky smile.

"I'm so glad that room is finished. If I had to paint one more ladybug, I was going to cry."

I laugh. "Well, it's all done. Plastic off the floor, rollers washed, pans thrown out. You don't have to worry about it anymore."

"Good. So, tell me," she says to me before taking a sip of her beer. "What now?"

"As far as I'm concerned? We live happily ever after."

34

QUINN

THIS MORNING I feel like a whole new person. My daughter thinks Brett is the best thing since sliced bread, and he adores her. I love Brett and he loves me, though we still have a lot to learn about one another. I actually felt like we were a family last night and that things were finally falling into place for me for the first time in years.

I did the right thing by letting Spencer go. Him changing was a pipe dream. I know now that I love Brett more than I ever loved Spencer.

When Spencer and I were at our happiest, we weren't actually happy. We just tolerated one another better and co-existed like roommates co-parenting a child, but there's something different about my and Brett's relationship.

There's an understanding of what the other has gone through. We appreciate what we have now, and I won't let anyone take that from me, and today even Thomas is a welcome knock at the door as Fran and I have coffee in the living room.

"Come in!" I yell, knowing it's him.

"Mmm, I smell coffee," he says, heading for the kitchen.

"Help yourself."

"I think I will."

"So, what brings you over so early this morning?" I ask.

"I figured maybe if we worked hard enough, we could knock out the rest of Evie's room today."

"It's already done," Fran laughs, pointing to Evie's room. Fran was the first one here this morning. Always the early bird.

Thomas peeks his head inside and Evie gives him a big hug. "Hey, Uncle Thomas!"

"Hey, Bug! How you liking your new room?"

"I love it!" With that, she runs back into her room, and I hear a thud as she jumps back onto her bed.

"You finished this all by yourself?" he asks me.

"No, Brett came over last night and helped." I try to say it nonchalantly, but I wince slightly because I still worry about how Thomas feels about my and Brett's relationship.

"No kidding? Well, that's amazing. He sounds like a good guy. I'd like to meet him."

"Oh, you can. His family is back from Malibu, and they've invited all of us to eat with them tonight at Brett's parents' house."

"Wow," Fran says, "that's awesome."

"Even me?" Thomas asks.

I laugh. "Well, of course even you. I can't leave out my best friend."

He claps his hands together. "Free food. I'm in."

He picks up his cup of coffee, and I relish the fact that Thomas and I seem to be back to normal. I don't fight it, and I welcome the sense of normalcy back in my life.

"You know, between everything that's happened, I still haven't unpacked my bags from the trip," I tell them.

"Honey, me neither," Fran says. "Unpacking seems like such a chore right now."

"Yeah, well, the next time you go to Malibu, remember to

invite me. I was completely lost with both of you gone," Thomas says, sipping his coffee.

"We'll make sure you go next time," I say with a wink.

———

TONIGHT, as I help dress Evie, Thomas and Fran get ready at my house, and I can already hear them fighting over the bathroom. Thomas is worse than a woman about looking pristine, especially his hair. I shake my head. I should have bought a place with two bathrooms. How will *I* ever get ready?

I manage. I do my makeup at my old vanity, which is nowhere near as nice as the one I used in Malibu. That thing must have cost a fortune. I shake the probable cost from my mind. Money is scary.

I take special care in my appearance today. Today this family meets the real me. No more engagements and no more hiding Evie. I smile at the thought that one day this could be Evie's family.

I've always wanted a big, close-knit family, and I hated that my daughter didn't have that luxury either. Maybe one day she will. I didn't have aunts and uncles to introduce her to or even grandparents. My parents were gone and Spencer didn't associate with his family. He left home when he was eighteen and has never been back.

I would tell Evie about my mother, though, and how much she would have loved her. I wanted her to feel like there were angels looking out for her, and if anyone were an angel, it would be my mother. I glance down at the heart ring that Brett bought me, which now sits in a dish, and I smile.

I want to wear it, but I'm not sure if it would be appropriate. Now I think that the ring was a sign from my mother that this is the man for me. I put the ring on, but on the opposite hand. I want to keep it with me always.

Sometime later, I'm finally allowed in my own bathroom to do my hair, and wouldn't you know it—Fran and Thomas start rushing me.

"We're supposed to be there in thirty minutes!" Fran calls out.

"What's taking her so long?" I hear Thomas ask.

I shake my head. It will always be like this with these two, but I smile because that's okay with me.

Brett calls to give me the address, having to work until it's time to be there, and Thomas, Fran, Evie, and I catch a cab to the house. When we arrive, the house is absolutely breathtaking. A two-story Victorian home with a wraparound porch. On the ceiling of the porch are fans and small, dimly lit chandeliers.

"This is beautiful," Fran breathes.

"Yes, it is," I agree.

Thomas just stands there in awe.

"This is the biggest house I've ever seen!" Evie exclaims.

"Hello, darling!" Kathryn calls out, reaching for me and pulling me into a hug.

"Hello, again, Kathryn. It's so good to see you. This is my friend, Thomas, and this is my daughter, Evie."

"Oh my, she looks just like you! Well, come in. Everyone is waiting on you. Brett should be here shortly. He got held up at the bar."

Thomas takes to the family like a fish to water, and Fran strikes up a conversation with Anne and Russ. Joe is his usual quiet self, but he peers around adoringly at his large family. I do, too. Evie is off playing in Nell's room, and I wait by the window for Brett.

"I'm so happy that you two worked things out," Kathryn says, handing me a cup of tea. "When you left, he was so lost."

"I'm sorry. I know I've caused your family a lot of trouble."

"No, dear. You didn't. I can get pretty forceful with my kids, and Brett did what he thought he had to do."

I chuckle lightly.

"What's so funny?"

"I was just thinking that your pushing Brett was apparently the right thing to do because without that push, he and I wouldn't have each other."

"Oh, I've never thought of it that way before. It's a beautiful way to think of it, isn't it?"

I nod and sip my tea. "Yes, it is."

"Well, we all know that a mother is always right." She winks.

"Most times," I say with a smile.

"He told me he loves your daughter. I told you he would understand. I know my son. You just had to give him a chance."

"I know that now, but everything worked out the way it was supposed to. I got all the answers I needed while we were apart."

"So, there are no more doubts?" she asks.

I shake my head. "No more."

"Good. Oh! There he is!"

I glance out the window and see my handsome boyfriend walking up the drive. My boyfriend. That sounds amazing. I don't need a husband or a sex buddy. I need a boyfriend.

He is the perfect boyfriend indeed. He's handsome, accomplished, and most importantly, he loves me and my daughter. He catches me spying on him from the drive and gives me the large smile that I've come to love and cherish.

"You're here," he says, kissing me as he enters.

"Where else would I be?"

"Did Fran and Thomas come?"

"Yep. They're in there with Anne and Russ. Is Phil coming?"

"Yeah, there he is now, actually." There, in a separate cab, is Phil, dressed to the nines, as always.

The house is jam-packed with family, friends, and enough food to feed a small army. Conversation and laughter are thick in the air. Brett never leaves my side, and Evie and Nell sit at the end of the mahogany dining table laughing as well. I peek around and it's then that it hits me.

I don't have to wish this were my family. It already is. I'm not going anywhere and neither is Brett. His family loves me, and I love them.

Fran leans over and whispers in my ear, "So, what do you wish for when you already have everything?"

I smile and whisper back, "I don't wish for anything anymore. I live in the now, and the now looks pretty good."

ABOUT THE AUTHOR

Jaime W. Powell is a full-time writer. She lives a quiet life in East Texas with her adoring husband, J.J., who is her best friend. Most days you can find her editing manuscripts for other talented authors or working on her next masterpiece.

For ten years, Jaime worked in the beauty industry in her hometown of Marshall, Texas. But after a particularly hard day at work, she sat down to write her first novel, Revamp. After completion, she put it on a shelf where it sat for eight years because she didn't believe anyone would take her writing seriously. Little did she know that book would become her first published novel and change her life forever.

From that moment on, she quit her job as a nail technician and dedicated herself to the literary industry completely which she has now made her home.

GREAT STORIES. NO GUILT.

www.cleanreads.com

CPSIA information can be obtained
at www.ICGtesting.com
Printed in the USA
FSHW021948101019
62916FS